MW00529753

RENTAL HOUSE

Also by Weike Wang

Joan Is Okay
Chemistry

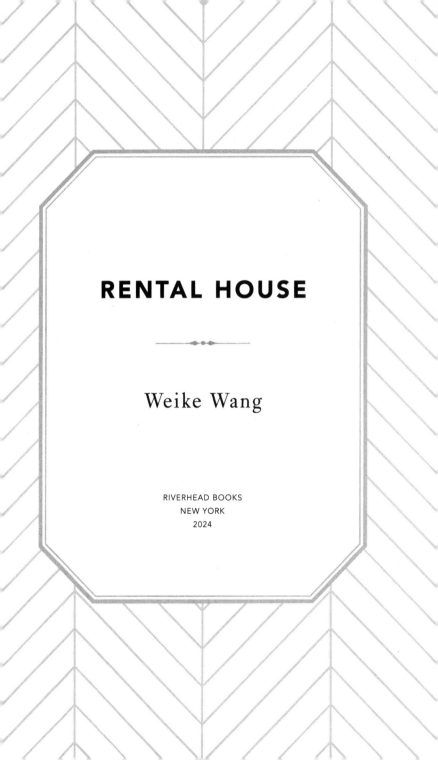

RENTAL HOUSE

Weike Wang

RIVERHEAD BOOKS
NEW YORK
2024

RIVERHEAD BOOKS
An imprint of Penguin Random House LLC
penguinrandomhouse.com

Library of Congress Cataloging-in-Publication Data
Names: Wang, Weike, author.
Title: Rental house / Weike Wang.
Description: New York : Riverhead Books, 2024.
Identifiers: LCCN 2023056709 (print) | LCCN 2023056710 (ebook) |
ISBN 9780593545546 (hardcover) | ISBN 9780593545560 (ebook)
Subjects: LCSH: Marriage—Fiction. | LCGFT: Novels.
Classification: LCC PS3623.A4585 R46 2024 (print) | LCC PS3623.A4585
(ebook) | DDC 813/.6—dc23/eng/20240104
LC record available at https://lccn.loc.gov/2023056709
LC ebook record available at https://lccn.loc.gov/2023056710

Printed in the United States of America
1st Printing

Book design by Nerylsa Dijol

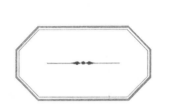

PART ONE

She had started looking in winter, browsing rental sites recommended by friends who went away for long periods of summer and knew about this stuff. They knew which towns along the Cape had the cleanest beaches, which towns on Nantucket were the most kid friendly, and which ice cream stands the Obamas frequented on the Vineyard. These tips she wrote down on a notepad. Martha's Vineyard = Obamas = ice cream. She'd marked kid-friendly places as ones to avoid. She and her husband of five years had discussed visiting the Cape before, but for five years had not. It was decided that this was the summer to do so. They would leave Manhattan and spend a month within walking distance of the Atlantic Ocean, in a classic New England cottage with gables, shutters, and two beds. Two beds so that both sets of parents could visit, staggered.

IN THE LEAD-UP WEEKS, Nate spoke of staying realistic. The year prior there'd been a pandemic. They'd forgone seeing parents or leaving the house much. He preferred the bubble but knew that bubbles had to be left. Soon, they were in a rental car, driving north. The trunk was full of food, clothes, cleaning supplies, and their gigantic four-year-old sheepdog, Mantou, sat upright in the back seat. While the idealistic vision of a trip with their parents had come from Keru, raising a full-size sheepdog in the city had been Nate's idea. A sheepdog fulfilled a boyhood dream. The pastoral one, of endless fields and a friend about your height whose fur your small hands could sink into and who could guide you into the magical woods. Nate had grown up in a small, one-story house with brown carpets. His mother had allowed two rats, many fish, a snake, but no dogs. "Those purebreds are expensive and bougie," she'd said. "Why waste money on them, when there are so many strays in need?"—none his mother ever took in.

About the name of their sheepdog, Keru and Nate had quarreled.

"Mantou means steamed bun," said Keru, who was bilingual and had left China as a youth.

"I know what it means," said Nate, who'd been taking Chinese lessons ever since he realized that whenever he was with Keru and her parents, he had no idea what was going on.

"So, what's wrong with Mantou?" asked Keru.

Nate brought up the propensity of yuppie couples to name their expensive dogs after basic starch items. The dog had come from a reputable breeder. They'd been two years on a waiting list and paid a not-insubstantial deposit to be on that list.

There was no fruit or vegetable Keru enjoyed enough to dedicate to their dog. She would also not be giving their dog a human name like Stacy. The other possibility was Huajuan, or a fancy-shaped, swirled steamed bun. Nate said the word a few times, believing that he was saying the word right, but Keru said that he was saying the word wrong, and though Nate couldn't hear where he'd gone wrong, and she couldn't explain exactly either, he agreed that Mantou was fine.

THE FIRST WEEK at the cottage was just them. Besides walking Mantou twice a day around the small, fenced neighborhood of other rental houses, Keru and Nate stayed in and binged real estate shows that featured multimillion-dollar properties. They talked about how crazy it would be to ever buy in their city, a city they both loved, but a city not without its problems, like cost, housing, hard-to-follow weekend transit updates, and a large, rich population that never took public transit and went on about how great and affordable the city was. Once Nate and Keru came out of that slump, they cooked easy meals with Hamburger Helper and drank copious amounts of gin. Whenever Mantou brought them a toy, they tossed it for her or played tug until she tired herself out. They had sex at random times of day, in various positions, sometimes with Keru's travel vibrator, which she would wrap in a sock and bury deep in their suitcase once parents were present. There was no street noise in Chatham. No constant chaos of being surrounded by human congestion. The silence became a topic of conversation—should a lack of sirens be in and of itself alarming, was everyone dead or well, and how do residents vent personal frustrations if they can't lay on the horn or scream?

Another topic was whose parents were more difficult. Each side made a strong case for their own, but this was pure anxiety talking and the answer didn't really matter.

The order of the visits was strategic. Keru's parents cared about cleanliness and personal safety to an obsessive-compulsive degree and, since the start of the pandemic, had yet to go outside without double masks, gloves, and Mace. If they had eaten out twice a year before, at the behest of Keru, who thought that an American family should, they would never do so again. They would never order takeout again either, and unless it was to see dying relatives or their own parents' graves, should China's borders ever fully reopen, they would never again board a plane. Keru's parents lived in central Minnesota, where Keru went to high school but did not consider home. To avoid spending a night in a motel, her parents drove to Chatham in shifts, stopping only at state-run rest stops, eating ramen noodles cooked in the car. They were visiting first, else they wouldn't have. They would have refused to stay in a cottage, in a bed slept in by some other couple, even if it was a couple they knew.

On their last night alone, Nate walked down the street to the local wine shop and bought a bottle of red for dinner. He would give Keru the option to get hammered, because once her parents arrived, she could not drink lest she risk their calling her an alcoholic. When he returned from the store, the whole place smelled, as expected, like bleach. Keru was in the bathroom scrubbing the grout and picking black specks off the ground. Then she was in the kitchen wiping water stains off the appliances. The dishes and utensils, which were already clean from the night before, she loaded into the dishwasher again and blasted them on high heat.

"Don't say we used the dishwasher," she said.

Nate had made that mistake before, in the first year of their marriage, letting it slip to his father-in-law, as a joke, that he and Keru ran the dishwasher nightly or sometimes just for fun.

"You're welcome to use that machine, Nate," his father-in-law had said formally, as if they were in court. "But Keru should not. To use a dishwasher is to admit defeat. No one is so busy that they can't take ten minutes out of their day to clean up their own mess. While you may not be industrious enough to use a sponge and detergent, Keru is, and you must encourage her to continue doing so."

This comment put Nate in a strange place. On one hand, his father-in-law had openly and casually called him inept; on the other, he also seemed to endorse Nate treating Keru like the help. Nate laughed nervously as his father-in-law watched. He learned that day that he and his father-in-law would not be friends, as he was with the dads of his previous girlfriends. He would not be drinking beer outside with him while grilling steak or fly-fishing or losing at cornhole. They would not be playing backgammon together or ribbing each other about useless trivia, and besides the well-being of Keru, they would share no common interests.

Nate asked Keru what she wanted to eat for dinner before her parents arrived with coolers of homemade food and there would be no choice.

Keru said she wasn't hungry, and the reason she wasn't hungry was that there was still so much to do. The trash and recycling bins were still full. She needed to launder all the sheets again, all the blankets, all the towels, hand towels, dish towels, wash the windows, mop the floors, sweep the driveway, lint roll herself, and do a last round of checks.

While his wife did some of that, Nate ate a granola bar with his hand cupped under his mouth. Then he uncorked the wine and set it on a napkin on the dining table, next to a single paper cup. He took Mantou out for her evening walk, down the unswept driveway, around the gravel path that led into a sand path that led down to a small beach. There were signs everywhere about dogs being on leash at all times, with "at all times" underlined and in bold font, but since the beach was empty, Nate let Mantou off for five minutes and watched her run toward the waves.

UPON ARRIVAL, Keru's parents took a brisk walk around the property. They commented on small imperfections like the narrowness of the driveway, the lack of a garden hose, should they need it to put out fires, should the house catch aflame. "Why would the house catch on fire?" Keru asked, and her mother listed possible reasons. Lightning, a fast-moving forest fire, neighbors not wanting them there, a leak in the gas line that either kills them in their sleep or leads to an explosion. Keru had heard many such lists before and had lists of her own. When she didn't look terrified enough, her mother pressed her index finger into the center of Keru's forehead and sent this forehead back. Nate's presence went mostly unacknowledged. Her parents waved to him from six feet away and have never touched his forehead or tried to, an arrangement he was okay with. From behind Nate, Mantou charged. When she leapt toward Keru's father, he dodged and said to Mantou in Chinese, "Not before we wash your paws." Once her parents deemed the area free of immediate threats, it was time to unload coolers, enter the cottage, unmask, and unglove. While Keru's mother prepared lunch, Keru's father brought out a basin of lukewarm water to clean each of Mantou's paws, for twenty seconds between each digit. Then he showed the brown water to Keru and Nate, who had insisted on paw wipes and no basin. Then Mantou was allowed back inside. After a lunch of cucumber salad and pork skewers, Keru's mother recruited Keru to wash dishes with her, and Keru's father recruited Nate to talk about fuel cells.

Keru's father worked in energy as an industry chemist, and Nate was an assistant professor who studied fruit flies. Both being men of science, it would seem that there could have been some overlap, but each time they met, the question his father-in-law opened with was whether there was any new research in biology or applied biology that could help with the current energy crisis, our inevitable withdrawal from fossil fuels, and the irreversible environmental damage caused already by billions of combustion engines. Fuel cells are the future, his father-in-law would say, lightly pounding his fist on something, like his other fist. Not nuclear or electric cars, not Elon Musk, but fuel cells that can convert hydrogen gas to current with zero emissions.

Nate hmm-ed and m-hmm-ed, then said, as he had the other times, that since he only studied flies, he knew of no recent advances that could help this future, though he felt bad for not being able to do so.

Nate used to think his father-in-law only spoke about fuel cells as a means to self-aggrandize. Then a few years back it occurred to Nate that maybe fuel cells were the only area that Keru's father felt proficient enough in to carry on a solo discussion in English that was reflective of his intellect. Her father had lots of company patents, lots of papers with long calculus and Greek symbols that Nate couldn't understand. With fuel cells, her father controlled the narrative and his own self-image. If this was the case, then Nate felt obliged to listen to him and to continue expressing, as an aspiring filial son-in-law, that he knew nothing about clean energy sources but was glad his father-in-law was working on the problem.

When Nate mentioned this fuel cell fixation to his mother as an anecdote, she didn't find it that funny and gave her opinion in the form of questions: "What do you mean that's all he talks to you about? He can't talk to you about anything else? Not the weather or your own work? Why does he expect you to get to know him but not the other way around?"

His mother usually called Nate from their landline in their cramped kitchen, hunched over a barstool, a stained apron around her waist but no food on the stove. While Nate and Keru were still dating, she also had questions: What kind of immigrants are they, what kind of Chinese people? Are they Christians? Do they believe in God? Did they enter the country the right way? Are her parents citizens? Is Keru a citizen? Do they feel more American or Chinese? Do they speak only Chinese around you? Do they know you don't understand Chinese? Have you asked? How is that offensive? You just explain, very politely, that we speak only English around Keru and expect Keru to speak only English with us.

The questions disappointed Nate, and he considered saying so except he also didn't want to hear her excuses for why xenophobia wasn't xenophobia. Like that she was Mama bear, and only asked hard-hitting questions for his own benefit, to help protect him (and them) from a parasitic foreign wife. The citizenship question was the one his mother asked most, and to help her disappoint him less, the only one he chose to answer. He explained the entire process. To become U.S. citizens, Keru and her parents had given up their red Chinese passports when Keru was not yet a teen. They'd taken a test, gone through interviews, pledged to the flag, been firmly handshaken and congratulated, you're now in the land of the free, which your former country was not. But even if Keru was not a citizen, even if she was still on a green card, or a visa, and their marriage would speed up the process, it didn't matter to him, he would marry Keru nevertheless. His mother said it didn't matter to her either, as long as Nate was happy. Three months later she asked about Keru's citizen status again, for she had forgotten what Nate had said. She promised to write it down this time, this answer that didn't matter to her.

His parents married straight out of high school, in the same church their parents had married in, in the same town they and their parents had been born in, at the foothills of the Blue Ridge Mountains. His mother waitressed until she got pregnant. His father managed a grocery store. When the grocery store went under, his parents moved to another town with another slightly worse store that needed to be managed. Summers and weekends, Nate worked the aisles, price-stickering cans of baked beans and pickles, putting orange sale tags on almost expired fruit pies. To discourage burglary, the tags' adhesive was impossibly strong. A thief would have to stand there for ten or more minutes, scraping at barcode labels, to be able take the produce out without setting off alarms. And that's the secret to discount retail, his father had taught him, as they stickered around old labels, using only a Sharpie to cross them out. His father worked from six to six on weekdays, on every Thanksgiving and Christmas, and had a 100 percent turnover of his staff each year. The younger generations irked him, and he was vocal about it, telling those who spent more time in the break room that they needed to step the hell up. When Nate was in high school, his father sat him down and said there was probably no future in grocery store management, hence Nate should seek out another path. He mentioned his sister's son, Nate's cousin, who worked in a tire factory a state over and was on the path to becoming a warehouse associate. He mentioned his other sister's son, who was in vocational school to be a welder.

"Any of that interest you?" his father asked.

Nate said he was open minded.

"A person should have skills," his father said, and while

Nate agreed, he also knew that his father meant physical skills. The loading and unloading of boxes. The working-with-your-hands type. Sports. Great but unspoken sadness descended on the household the day Nate announced he would stop trying out for their school's basketball, football, or baseball teams. At least his older brother, Ethan, had wrestled, but Nate had grown long and thin. In full-length mirrors, he sometimes mistook himself for a toothpick.

When Yale accepted Nate on full financial aid—a surprise to everyone, since no one knew that he'd applied or that such schools offered aid—his mother went to the nicest store in their town, a Sears, and bought his first real winter coat, filled with synthetic down. It was a size too big, but his mother said he would grow into it, which he never did. At Yale, Nate met Keru at a Halloween party during their senior year. She had shown up to this party in a leopard-print turtleneck, a plaid jacket, and shiny gold pants. He had shown up with a shark fin strapped to his back.

"What are you supposed to be?" he asked.

"Indecision," she said. "Or a bad dress day. Why? What are you supposed to be?"

He pointed to his silly foam fin and wiggled himself foolishly. "Can't tell? A great white."

She shot him an incisive look. Next, she laughed, like really laughed. Because she thought his costume was making a clever aquatic pun on being another well-to-do Caucasian male at an Ivy League school. He said he hadn't meant to be that clever. He was taken aback and embarrassed. She laughed some more.

Since this was still a party, he let the laughing girl assume things about him. He didn't announce right away that he was a poor white from nowhere and the first in his family to go to college. There were acronyms for people like him now, support groups and mentors. The first time he heard the term *first gen*, he was the new assistant professor on a new committee for how the school could better support these kids. What were their needs? What was the transition? Until then, Nate hadn't thought about his own needs or transition, and had his brother Ethan gone to college, Nate wouldn't have needed to be the first. But Ethan had met the wrong people, stolen some cars, and spent a semester in juvie. Upon release, he finished high school, then drove west, south, then back west, finding work where he could. Nate knew little of Ethan's whereabouts, except when the occasional letter arrived confessing a newfound love for Jesus so could Nate please send some money to facilitate his new religiosity, preferably hundred-dollar bills wrapped in tissue paper to this random address. When Nate confronted their mother about the letters (he knew she was sending Ethan the money and had also forwarded Ethan his New Haven address), she reminded Nate that he should stop letting elitist ideas get the better of him, that he and Ethan were cut from the same cloth, had been loved the same, been gifted with the same proclivities, and only by God's will was Nate now on a different path, and the outcomes could have been reversed.

While his mother was not a deeply religious woman and loathed going to church on Easter, so did not, she deployed "by God's will" whenever she needed to wrestle control of a conversation and end it. His mother knew Nate no longer believed in God. She used to want to know why. No specific reason, he said honestly, it just stopped making sense to him, gradually, not all at once. His mother said she didn't understand, and Nate said, "Mom, given that faith has been and is used to justify any number of acts, it seems ultimately self-serving"—though he could see its benefits with regard to providing personal comfort and structure. His mother still didn't understand, and Nate said that with faith you eventually hit a wall, and while he could see people coming to it through, say, Pascal's wager, he would go on without it and just strive to be a decent person.

His mother's face seemed to shrivel and cave in. "Wall?" she muttered. "Wager?" She became stoic and took a moment.

"Don't forget from where you came," she said, and Nate said he hadn't, and his father said, "You have, and look, now you've upset your mother," who, after concluding that Nate had no good reason not to believe in God, had begun to cry.

So Nate chose not to talk about his brother or these family dynamics. Sometimes he just let others assume that he came from well-to-do Caucasians and was an only child.

Keru was an only child and had come to the Halloween party alone, on a whim, to make her senior year less intense.

"Some people say they're scared of me," she said. "Boo," she said, and he jumped.

He was scared but also intrigued. He imagined the first scientists felt the same when they stumbled across electricity.

Soon, they found a sofa to occupy, and as Nate was telling her how he was off to grad school next year to study simple organisms, Keru picked up a coaster from the messy coffee table and flung it across the room into the crowd, without breaking eye contact with Nate or acknowledging the act.

"Did you just?" he asked, pointing after the thrown object.

"Do what?" she said.

She picked up another coaster and as she rolled it across her knee, he retracted his finger and asked about her postgrad plans.

"Not med school," she said, rolling the coaster.

"Not law school," she said, sailing the coaster across the room, like a Frisbee.

"Not finance," she said, reaching for the empty Solo cup (there were no more coasters).

"Which leaves only one possible option," she said.

"Uh," he said, having fallen into a stupor.

"Consulting?" she asked, then seeing him unresponsive, asked, "Have you heard of it?" then seeing him still unresponsive, said, "Like eighty hours a week, meals delivered to your desk, highly urgent but ultimately meaningless consulting."

About 70 percent of their graduating class went into consulting. At freshman orientation, they were invited to recruitment season.

Once he collected himself, he nodded and said, "Yes, ma'am." Then he placed a hand on his flushed cheek. "Sorry. You're making me nervous."

Her smile was genuine, warm and mischievous, as if after she finished smiling she would either strike or hug him.

She leaned in closer and told him she had a secret that could make him more nervous. He leaned in as well and asked what it was. The secret was that she intended to unapologetically make money. "I have no family connections or generational wealth. But I'm determined to build a life worth the trials it took my parents and me to get here. You with me, Nate the great white?"

He wondered if by "You with me" she meant "Do you understand the words coming out of my mouth," or "Are you ready to join my cause?" Keru blinked much less than an average human and much less than he did. After the Solo cup, she threw a mechanical pencil. After the mechanical pencil, she threw a spiral-bound notepad. They heard someone yell "Hey, what the fuck" but the party kept going, the music kept playing, until at the end of the night, Nate asked Keru if he could see her again, and she glanced away from him at the now, finally, cleared coffee table, and said "Maybe."

NATE KNEW ENOUGH Chinese to follow the conversation but not enough to contribute. Since most of his brain was already dedicated to listening and translating, no cells remained for the construction of original thought. His Chinese teacher had said he was at the stage of second-language learning she called monotasking. "Many people never get past this stage," she warned, and encouraged him to take the leap into active conversation. "Just leap?" "Yes, leap now!" His logic was disjointed, his fragments nonsensical. As he babbled, white foam pooled at the corners of his mouth. Soon, his teacher told him to stop leaping, he wasn't a frog.

These weekly lessons weren't fun and reminded him that his prior second-language learning had been a joke. He'd taken eight years of Spanish in total, earning As each semester, and he knew no Spanish. He knew more Chinese now out of necessity. Nate's teacher was from Beijing and spoke with a prideful precision that was militant. On their first day, she had yelled at him, but then he realized that was her natural way of speech. She'd yelled, "Mandarin is spoken by one point four billion people and is the most spoken language in the world." She'd yelled, "English is spoken by only six hundred million, but with English and Mandarin, you're able to communicate with two billion people in this world, isn't that wonderful?" Nate said he didn't need to communicate with that many people, he just needed to communicate with his in-laws. When the teacher learned that Keru and her family were from southwest China, from farmland, she explained that they spoke a dialect of Mandarin that was flatter, rounder, and ultimately less precise. Dialects such as these, of the rural peoples, can be grouped under the umbrella term *tu hua*, or "talk of the dirt." "I can't teach you talk of the dirt," she'd admitted but then added that finding a teacher who could was impossible. Beijing Mandarin is the official language; dialect is what you speak at home. So, without other viable options and because Keru was an unwilling teacher, Nate learned the government-sanctioned Mandarin from a paid professional and tried to apply that to what he heard within his wife's household, an exercise that was like shoving a square peg into a round hole, but with enough force, and with every neuron dedicated to the problem, he could smash the square peg through.

But from the outside, this feat of comprehension didn't look like much. He sat and listened. He assumed a dopey expression and was mute.

The week was spent indoors and around meals. Each morning, at breakfast, Keru's parents confronted them with an array of meat and spinach buns, scallion pancakes, waffles, and an assortment of fluids. Each morning, they had to finish it all, else, her parents warned, they would have no energy for the day and pass out. While they ate to ward off fainting, Keru asked her parents if they actually wanted to go anywhere today. Like the beach. Or a drive along the famous seashore. Tons of lighthouses. And they didn't even need to get out of the car, they could just admire the structures from afar, with all the windows up and through the tinted glass.

Her parents shook their heads in unison.

"Too many people," her father said. They'd seen the sand dunes on their drive here, and he imagined sand looked pretty much the same across the board.

Would they at least consider coming out with them for a walk? asked Keru. It was good weather again, as it had been yesterday and the day before, low humidity, fluffy clouds. At the word *walk*, Mantou barreled in from the living room to flop down by the breakfast table, by her father's feet. Her father tried to pet Mantou but couldn't find a perfect spot so hovered his hand above the black-and-white fur as the dog flailed from neglect. Keru's parents were not animal people, though as a boy, Keru's father had raised dogs to guard property and crop fields. They were not the kind to pet or live inside. Keru's mother had been afraid of dogs, especially large ones that could jump and put their paws on your shoulders. When Mantou had done that to Keru's mother, she stumbled back, screaming. Then she screamed at Keru for almost killing her.

The jumping was trained out of Mantou, but another year had to pass before Keru's mother would agree to be in the same room as the dog. She wondered aloud to her husband, with Keru present, if Keru had gotten a dog to ostracize her own mother. Keru had known of her mother's dog phobia, and Keru now had a giant dog. Here was where Nate could see his in-laws' difficulties. They could speak about Keru as if she were not there and spin all sorts of hypotheticals about why she had not been more conscientious. When Nate said the sheepdog had been his initiative, to fulfill a boyhood dream, his in-laws thanked him for sharing his wonderful dream but continued to theorize that Keru must have put him up to saying that, so as to divert blame.

Nonetheless there was fondness now between dog and parents, and often Keru's father called Mantou the great big panda dog.

Though immediately after stroking the great big panda dog he would go to the sink and wash his hands.

Two years into the pandemic, few people remained as vigilant as Keru's parents. Yet on the other end of that spectrum were Nate's parents, who had refused to vaccinate, and when they contracted the virus, refused to admit that they had it or to quarantine. For six months, his father lost his sense of smell and blamed allergies. His mother had severe muscle pains but declined to test or take Tylenol. Over the phone, Nate asked how they ever expected to travel to places like New York, say, to visit him and Keru, if they ignored each and every guideline. His mother said, "Then we won't travel, we'll wait it out, one day science says one thing, the next another." Nate reminded her that he was a scientist. "Which we're very proud of," she said, but whatever science he believed in, he should also know when to keep it to himself. She wasn't pushing her science onto him; she wasn't telling him what to do. Nate explained that there was no his or her science, no one owned that word, and more importantly, she and his father weren't scientists, had not gone to school to study it, taken qualifying exams, defended a thesis that took six years to complete, done three more years of a postdoc, and was now finally on a tenure track that would take another seven years because of bureaucracy, grant funding, and because fruit-fly research was so fucking slow—since you actually had to grow the flies and catch them, and if you're trying to study the social patterns among colonies, you had to observe for hours at a time, months. His final remark to his mother was "our opinions are not worth the same," after which the line went quiet. Nate thought she'd either set the phone down or hung up. Then he heard, "You forget who you're talking to, Nathan. I am your mother and we shall not discuss this anymore."

That Nate's parents had never been keen on him entering science Keru could not comprehend. "Who wouldn't want their child in science?" she'd asked. "Or health care? You can always get a job as a doctor. There will always be a need for scientists."

Except those like Nate made a fraction of a doctor's salary and did work no layman could understand. "Why not law?" his parents had suggested, each semester he'd spent at Yale and each summer he returned. "Doesn't Yale have a law school and won't it be nice to have a lawyer in the family?" From law, he could find his way into politics, the senate, the presidency, or maybe even the Supreme Court.

Keru blinked as if coming out of a coma. These were possibilities totally off-limits to someone like her.

"But not off-limits to me," he'd said. And not just off-limits, but wide open, run for office, Nate, be the voice of the people, and had he any interest in representing his people, he could see his own appeal. From Appalachia to the Ivy League. From white trash to the White House. "You're not white trash," Keru had said. He asked her what she thought white trash was, and she couldn't say, except, "That's not you."

Nate had finished his share of the breakfast when Keru's mother brought out another tray of steamed buns. He picked one up robotically and tore at its bouncy, white skin to reveal the black, red bean center. The conversation between Keru and her parents had veered into the technical, and unable to follow its logic entirely, Nate followed his wife's face. It had changed from spirited optimism to a blank sheet of paper. There was a sequence of topics her parents preferred. First, careers, at what point in the near future would Nate get tenure and Keru make partner. "TENURE" and "PARTNER," her father boomed in English, and nodded at his son-in-law until Nate nodded back. Second, finances and her father's position on how best to save money. The gist was, You can't keep renting forever, Keru. You should learn how to pay off a mortgage and be a real adult. Then, kids? When are you going to have those? Your mother plans to be a grand-mother and having kids is the socially responsible thing to do, even if the process depletes you. Once kids entered the conversation, so did Keru's mother, who wrung her hands and said it was Keru's father who plans to be a grandparent, not her. She supported whatever choice Keru made as long as she made the decision herself, had no regrets, and didn't expect childcare from her.

"I will not move closer to you to take care of your child," her mother said. "That is something I definitely will not do."

Her father told Keru not to put off child-rearing for the cost. "Yes, kids are expensive, and you alone probably cost us hundreds of thousands of dollars, but don't let that stop you, don't overthink it. Should you need more money, we can help."

In response, Keru's mother punched her husband on the arm. "What's the point of teaching our daughter how to manage money if you're just going to offer her ours for free? Only Chinese kids expect their parents to bankroll them; American kids do not. Take Nate, for example." On cue, she gestured to him, as if to say, there you are, Nate, thanks for sitting there like a statue and eating as you were instructed, now please stay as you were while I applaud your Western virtues in front of my Chinese daughter. On cue, Nate straightened, stuffed the rest of the steamed bun into his mouth, and strained to decode what good things were being said about him.

"Nice American boy who never asks his parents for money and makes his own way through life. Keru could learn from him. Nate worked minimum-wage jobs all through high school. Keru never had to do that."

The East versus West binary was, of course, not true. Had Keru been given a choice, she might have worked for minimum wage in high school instead of studying for zero dollars an hour. Had Nate's parents had any money, he would have asked for it.

Keru said nothing. Most people were scared of her, but she was scared of her parents.

"Nate doesn't really want to live in New York, does he?" her mother asked. "He only lives there because Keru makes them. Because Keru is bossy. What's so great about a city with an old train system, a homeless problem, and violent crimes on the news every night?"

There were lots of great things about the city in terms of culture, which her parents didn't care for, in terms of cuisine variety, which her parents didn't bother with, but even Nate had to admit that the most unfathomable crimes he'd ever heard came from channel 1 news. Crimes like random shootings and random stabbings, collateral damage in the form of dead children, crimes like severed body parts found in suitcases, the pushing of people down trash chutes, crazy people on the subway demanding crazy things of the sane riders, and once, the smearing of feces into a woman's face, a woman who was simply waiting for the train. He attributed these acts to population density. The more people packed into a place, the more erratic the behavior. But he knew Keru's mother didn't buy this argument, for she had grown up in the densely populated city of Changsha, population eight million, and had never encountered crimes like these. The day an Asian woman was pushed in front of a subway train to her death by a stranger, her mother called Keru continuously until she picked up. She demanded Keru boycott subways altogether, and Keru said she couldn't do that since her firm was too far downtown from their apartment.

"Then bring Nate with you at all times," replied her mother.

"Like in my pocket?"

"No, make him stand in front of you. Or behind you."

"Nate has to work too."

"But he won't get pushed in front of a train," her mother reexplained. "You married him for a reason. Use him as a shield."

In the real world, Nate would gladly be the shield, but in front of his in-laws, he straddled the line between siding with their daughter or letting her be. To avoid seeming like *that* guy, neutrality was preferred. These were her parents and, as Keru believed, the only people on Earth who could talk to her like this. The three of them had journeyed through something together, and for many years, despite driving one another mad, they were her only home. Keru had no other relations in America. No grandparents, aunts, uncles, or cousins on the same continent. Nate could not grasp that, really. To never be able to say, *Got into it with Mom again, Spending the night at my aunt's,* or *My cousin's a real dickhead but he's in town and wants to hang,* or *Granddad's back in the hospital and it's not looking good, so we'll all drive down to see him.* For three out of four grandparents, Keru didn't fly back in time. She texted her cousins on and off, but was teased and then ignored for having Chinese stuck in the '90s, which it was, since her speech patterns mimicked those of her parents, who'd left China in the '90s. Nate knew these facts of Keru's life but still could not imagine having gone through it. Americans liked to tout that the country was built by immigrants and is a melting pot of their descendants, but so far removed from this experience were most Americans, was his own family by at least four generations, what did it really mean to him? There had been no immigrant enclave in his town. He had not tasted sushi until college.

As breakfast went on, Nate felt he and Keru had been tied to a pole, with their backs together, in a basement filling with smoke. "Could we please be excused?" did not work with Keru's parents. There were no boundaries within this family, no line that could not be crossed, and if one parent had an opinion, it would have to be aired. A recent murder in Chinatown was brought up. Atrocious. Senseless. Nate had forced himself to watch the entire surveillance video of an unsuspecting young Asian woman stalked from floor to floor, down narrow corridors, by a hooded man no more than a few feet behind.

"She was found topless in her own bathtub," said Keru's mother. "Followed into her own apartment by a Black man and stabbed forty times. Her last moments were spent in horror. She could have been you, and think of her mother who came all the way here to build a better life for her child, only to have her die that way without cause."

Because Keru had been eating her upper lip, a small corner of her mouth started to bleed. She dabbed at it with a finger, then wiped the finger on a napkin. By emphasizing the word for "black" or *hei*, Keru's mother was expressing a view that Nate found increasingly hard to ignore. No euphemistic phrase for dark skin existed in Chinese, and when Keru tanned in the summer, her mother would remark on how *hei* her skin was and how careless she was to have let herself be made black by the sun, *shai hei*. Her parents were well into their sixties. They were not going to change. While they hadn't grown up with diversity, while China suffered greatly during the opium wars, spheres of influence, the taking and giving back of Hong Kong, and the persistent anti-China sentiments in the West, they still believed, thanks to relentless conditioning, that light skin was better and most white people were good. "I can't ignore that," Nate had said, to which Keru outstretched her arm and welcomed him to be the beacon of wokeness for her parents, an open position that he could fill with his innate ethnical goodness, since being their daughter was hard enough. "I'm just one person," she said. "I can't do it all."

When Nate raised his hand to speak, the rest of the table pivoted to him. In stunted Chinese, he said of the Chinatown killer that his brain was not there. He did not say Black man, he just said man. Then Nate gestured to his own temple, but he could hear the tonal mistakes as he made them. Maybe he said brain. Or maybe he said bath towel.

"What?" asked Keru's mother.

"He was mentally unwell," Nate said in English. At once, he hated himself. Fluency as a weapon.

Keru's mother's head tucked back into her neck, giving her a slight double chin. She glared at her daughter and didn't talk to Nate anymore. Keru's father sighed. No one moved. Once the pause became unbearable, Keru managed to get out, "If not New York, then where would we live?"

"Where?" her mother said a little louder.

"Anywhere," her father said even louder.

"Minnesota," her mother yelled.

In Minnesota, Keru's parents kept to themselves and had few friends. They lived just outside of St. Cloud, in a township that crossed miles of level farmland. The first time Nate visited, Keru's father drove him and Keru around; though she had not wished to come, her father insisted in case he or Nate required a translator. Nate watched Keru stare out the window, resigned, while Keru's father spoke proudly of Minnesota and taught Nate that this state, which Nate had never spent much time thinking about, was in the Corn Belt, the Dairy Belt, and the frost belt, what a diversity of geographical belts to experience, just like the diversity of America. Then Keru's father spoke about how the area reminded him of his hometown—inland and agrarian—as did the people. In Chinese, he instructed Keru to "tell Nate about my hometown."

She turned to Nate and said her father's hometown was geographically in the center of China, and it was, similarly, very flat, like you could walk miles and miles and not escape it, like the world was actually flat there, and there was a lack of dimensionality, a lack of texture or fullness, an absence of change, which is how a person not from the Midwest might feel living with her parents in the Midwest. Keru's father nodded, though not quite clear on what her daughter had said.

Their closest neighbor in Minnesota ran a dairy farm. He'd told Keru's father that he had four daughters when he needed four sons. "You need sons to do the milking," he'd said, and Keru's father nodded knowingly, for he had grown up in Hunan with two brothers, three sisters, and their father relied on the boys for the harvest, but on the girls (and their delicate hands) for the planting. Keru's father and this neighbor had exciting chats about baling hay, and on baling day, her father went over to help. In return, he was gifted a gallon of fresh milk that he gladly took, without mention that he and his wife were lactose intolerant.

Beyond this neighbor, Keru's parents spoke of few other acquaintances. They did not visit county fairs, follow hockey, attempt to ice climb, snowmobile, snowshoe, head "up north," go tubing, fishing, boating, speak Minnesotan, eat Jell-O salads or hot dish, listen to Prince (know who Prince is), comprehend Paul Bunyan (some giant man with an axe that somehow doesn't get caught in his beard), or appreciate *Fargo* (understand *Fargo*). When Keru was still in the school system, they excluded themselves from all parental obligations and events. But obvious facts about the state they could appreciate. The cost of living was low, there was space, big sky, lots of shopping plazas and strip malls, lots of parking, friendly Canada just northward should U.S.-China relations implode or climate change destroy the Midwest. In Minnesota, you could buy your food and toilet paper in bulk. You could get milk from your neighbor whose skin was ruddy and sunburnt, but ultimately, in winter, the color of churned butter, and you could go days without seeing a brown person or another Asian. Her parents had voluntarily left a place of many Asians for a place with few. In their minds, too many Asians in an area was not ideal, and could only draw dissent or hate from the locals, as in *Look, here comes another overqualified Asian to steal a specialized job that no one really wants.*

After that breakfast, Keru spent a long time in the bathroom with the door closed. When she came out, she told Nate they should walk the dog. Keru's father was clearing the table and wiping it down. Keru's mother was at the sink, washing the dishes and then the sink.

"See you, panda dog," Keru's father said with a gentle wave as they harnessed Mantou.

"Be good, Mantou," Keru's mother said as they walked out the door.

ON THE SECTION of beach with no one else around, Nate let the dog off while Keru sat in the sand, then lay down on the sand, like a starfish. Her eyes were closed. She was taking deep breaths. It was like that for a while, Nate in between his sad starfish and their happy dog, when a woman from the other end of the beach, three hundred or so feet away, started calling out to them. She was older, blond, and wrapped in an embellished white shawl, beige linen pants, strolling down the shoreline barefoot, toward them. Nate pretended not to notice her or hear what she was saying. The woman moved closer until her singsong voice became hard to ignore. "Hi, excuse me. Hello. Yes, you two. Your dog. There are signs. Let's heed the rules and do our part." Mantou was already in the water, breaking through waves. The woman pointed at Mantou and made exaggerated expressions of alarm. Nate signaled an apology to her and was about to get Mantou when Keru opened her eyes and sat up. She reached for the nearest large rock, and, in the woman's general direction, flung it. The rock landed a few feet in front of her, kicking up sand. The woman stopped to gawk at the small crater and, a second later, to shriek. The shrieks were discordant and annoying. Mantou stopped plowing through the ocean and pointed her entire body at the shrieking woman, as if she were a squeaky ball in need of being fetched. Nate called for Mantou to come here. As he leashed up their dog, Keru found the second-largest rock and held it in her hand. She looked calmly at the woman until she stopped screaming and looked at Keru in horror. Then the woman took a few steps backward, before turning around to walk away.

INSTEAD OF GOING to bed early as they usually did, on their last night in Chatham Keru's parents sat with her, Nate, and Mantou in the living room to watch that real estate show about luxury properties. For a few episodes, the show went to France and followed expat couples who were permanently resettling in Paris. Why expat and not immigrant, a question Keru had posed to Nate long ago when he used the word to describe college friends who had moved to Asia, on scholarships, to teach children there English despite not knowing the native language spoken by everyone else in that country. Nate doubled down that his friends were expats, not immigrants, and this led to a heated discussion that characterized the early years of their dating—the aggressive comparison of their worldviews, which ultimately led to clarifications in their basic English vocabularies. Expats left wealthy nations to humble themselves at the altar of the world, immigrants escaped poorer nations to be the workforce of the rich. For Nate, the word *immigrant* sat closer to migrant or refugee, and though an expat did move overseas for work opportunities, much like immigrants, the term also seemed to imply vacation and adventure, enjoyed by a person such as himself.

On screen, a French real estate agent walked through each listing with the expat couple, and in each room asked the pair how they felt about the energy of the space. Then they went to a nearby café to solidify these feelings over coffee and fresh croissants. That no one was discussing the actual price or size of the property left Keru's father in a state of agitated disbelief. These numbers were flashed across the screen but not dwelled upon. The expat wife wanted lots of sunlight. The expat husband wanted city center, in addition to sunlight. "But what about price per square feet?" Keru's father asked no one. "What about value? The sun will always be there." From the lounge chair, he converted each property's square meter to square foot in his head and announced it. Then he calculated the cost per square foot and announced it. Keru's mother liked some of the penthouse terraces, but said all the places were in areas with too many people, too many cars, and she'd heard from a friend who'd been to Paris that the French did not like Asians. They liked that Asians bought their overpriced bags, shoes, perfume, and clothes. They liked that Asians considered French culture the pinnacle of European elegance, but they did not think the same of Asians, especially not of Chinese tourists, whom they mocked for being loud and uncouth, despite wanting to siphon off all their money.

"I don't think that's true," said Keru.

"It's not?" asked Keru's mother. "Then why are you watching this show?"

"*We* are watching the show," said Keru. The word for "we" in Chinese is *wo men*, and if said quick enough, sounded like "women."

"Nineteen sixty-two square feet," said Keru's father. Then: "Twelve seventy-seven euros per square feet or thirteen eighty-six dollars, not considering closing costs."

Nate checked the math on his phone calculator. It was all correct. Keru shared her father's mental acuity, and Nate had seen them compete over mental math—who could tally up the bill fastest, who could convert large distances, who could make the best estimate. "It used to embarrass me," Keru had told Nate. "But now I like it. I see what he was training me to do." Once Nate had sat at the exit of a grocery store for half an hour, waiting, while father and daughter stood in front of the gumball machine and argued about how many gumballs were inside. The volume of the glass globe divided by each volume of the gumball, yet how to account for the empty space? They each had their theories.

As the night wore on, Keru and her mother continued to disagree about city versus countryside, interior design choices, the paradox of Asian wealth versus exclusion, and the dubious work ethic of French real estate agents.

Keru's mother: "They make deals look too easy. They dress too well. They eat at least three meals a day. Where's the suffering? Show me the suffering."

Keru: "Why must there always be suffering? I know we're immigrants, so we suffer, but why must we bear witness to it at all times?"

"Because suffering is required," replied Keru's mother. "To suffer is to strive and to set a bar so high that one never becomes complacent. To become complacent is to become lazy and to lose one's spirit to fight, and to lose one's spirit to fight is to die. So, to suffer is to live."

The way Keru's mother spoke Chinese was without verbal fillers or pauses.

Keru tried to make the argument that some cultures prefer to project ease, while others do not.

"Ease is an illusion," said her mother. "Nothing worth achieving can or should be easy, and if you chose to do something for its ease, then you have become complacent."

"Are we complacent?" her mother asked when Keru had no follow-up.

Keru shook her head.

"Am I right?" her mother asked.

Keru sighed.

"Am I right?"

"You're right," Keru said, and her mother nodded.

The way Keru's mother spoke to Keru was how Nate's Chinese teacher spoke to him, so now he understood.

The way Keru's father spoke to Keru was how coaches spoke to athletes, so now he understood.

The attitude that Keru's parents and to an extent Keru held toward suffering was, at first, hard to understand, but then one day, Nate saw its parallel in religious guilt, which he understood very well—the fundamental belief that a person could seek to be good but never quite achieve it or be deserving of better. The belief that to live was to struggle, and that to struggle was a given, yet one need not know why.

Neither Keru nor Nate struggled to feed, clothe, or shelter themselves. They saved most of their joint income and budgeted accordingly. But a habit Keru could not kick was gravitating to coupon stacks or the clearance racks at grocery stores. When she still lived with her parents in the Midwest, they bought absolutely nothing at full price and selecting the least-near-expired product from a sales bin was a skill. That Keru no longer needed to do that caused her significant discomfort. Nate had seen Keru scold herself. In the checkout line at Whole Foods, she would scan their cart and say, "We've spent more in a week than my father used to make in a month. I don't even buy items on sale anymore. I've forgotten the struggle."

"But it's not that I've forgotten," Keru would reply to herself. "Why suffer more than I have to? Why keep asking myself if I've suffered enough?"

"Who are you talking to?" Nate would ask.

"My mother, who else?"

When one episode of the real estate show ended, another began. A new expat couple was introduced, ready to find the chateau of their dreams, and despite the overt, self-indulgent messaging—immigration can truly be bliss if you have unlimited resources—no one suggested they watch something else or that it was time to turn in. Mantou snored from her dog bed, her limbs bunched together in a position that Nate called the Most Adorable. Keru and her mother had moved closer on the couch. They had the same smile, but without the smile Keru looked like her square-jawed father, who continued to hold great posture from his lounge chair, with both arms on the armrests, as if ready to be interviewed by the television or awaiting a glass of rare scotch that he would never have drunk.

"I like that backsplash," Keru said.

"I don't dislike it entirely," her mother replied.

"Thirty-two forty square feet," her father said. "Fifteen twenty euros per square feet or sixteen sixty-nine dollars rounded up."

NATE THOUGHT the visit went better than average. To be with his in-laws was to watch his wife turn into someone else, and logically he knew why it happened and why it had to. The role of daughter could not go unfulfilled, and his in-laws did not see him as a real son. Around him, they were performative, nice. He was like the store clerk at their favorite T.J. Maxx, a person they recognized and smiled at, but ultimately not one they needed to mind. Around Keru, they could be themselves and heap on to her their innumerable biases and judgment. She was their built-in translator and listening board. She was not expected to have opinions of her own. In turn, she absorbed their anxieties and complaints, mirrored their verbal tics, and regressed to a childlike state that only encouraged her parents to continue their campaign.

"At least you didn't cry," he told her as they stood in the driveway, waving to her parents' car as it grew smaller and smaller, then made a turn.

"I don't usually cry," she said.

"Last time you cried."

"Not in front of them."

Last time was before the pandemic. They'd rented a house, equidistant between them, in the middle of Ohio.

On the map, Keru's father had measured equal mileage, equal time spent on the road, equal gas cost, approximately. Nate understood less Chinese that time, but he remembered a dinner in which everyone was talking, perhaps even positively, and then Keru stopped talking and only her parents were talking at her, less positively, until the food got cold. Keru held it in for two more days, but the moment she and Nate left the house, the moment their car got out of the driveway, she rolled down the windows and cried. What had happened? She now couldn't exactly remember. Except the visit had probably been a shit show and her parents had probably been difficult. She could recall the feeling, though, that of her core being excavated with two metal claws. Once the claw-parents left, that hole in her chest, huge and gaping, would gradually fill again as she lived her own life, made her own choices. Then, the next visit would come and it would be excavated again. Not that her parents were unfeeling machines, no, and that she even thought to liken their attention to claws only amplified her guilt. For almost two decades, they had been her sole guardians and protectors. They made the most of what they had but were so sorely underequipped during her childhood that she didn't have a childhood, but then again neither had they. She and her parents had a finite amount of time left together, and from now until one of their deaths, that time would be cut up and concentrated into these tiny bursts. She wanted these bursts to be laced with happy memories, yet the three of them seemed unable to pull it off. Possibly because none of them really believed in happiness. They believed in unhappiness because they had lived it. To be unhappy together was a comfort.

MOST PEOPLE WANTED to know what her name meant. "Such a pretty name," Nate's mother had said when they first met at one of Yale's graduation events, an outdoor picnic luncheon to which most of the mothers showed up in floral dresses and floppy sun hats.

"How do you tell any of them apart?" Keru asked Nate as they walked through a set of gothic iron gates, Nate a few steps ahead, his hands in his khakis, his white oxford shirt half wrinkled and untucked. He lifted his chin toward a tall, slightly overweight woman wrapped in yellow chrysanthemums. She had already claimed a spot in the shade, at the end of a table, and had already fetched three glasses of pink lemonade. Alone, she hunched her broad shoulders together, as if to seem small. When she saw them, she expanded her chest and began patting the table with both hands.

As always, Keru introduced herself as Keru like Peru.

"Such a pretty name. It must mean something."

"It doesn't," Keru replied, and then took a sip of the lemonade that was so oversweetened, the pieces of granulated sugar scraped down her throat.

Her future mother-in-law seemed unconvinced. Up

close, her hair was the color of wet hay. She had very thin lips that, when pressed together, folded back into her mouth and disappeared.

"Eventually you'll have to tell me," she said, either a finger wag in her voice or a wink. "Nathan doesn't mean anything. It's just his father's middle name."

Nate asked where his father was.

His mother ignored the question.

She asked Nate to point out which buildings he had lectures in.

He said they weren't in this area. They were elsewhere.

She asked Nate to point in the direction of elsewhere.

He did, but aimlessly, and had his mother walked in the direction of his finger, she would have ended up nowhere.

Then she asked Nate to tell her what that building was, the one right in front of them with red brick and black shutters.

She asked about each adjacent building and those behind.

She asked where the law school was, and Nate said "That way," which was not the way to the law school.

Nate's mother soon assumed the role of indefatigable cheerleader, and Keru lost count of the number of times Nate was told that he made them proud. He accepted these accolades casually, and Keru felt bad that all his mother got in exchange was sugary lemonade and wrong directions.

Later, Nate learned that his father had been parking.

For two hours, he had been circling campus unable to find a spot large enough that did not require a delicate maneuver to get in. Keru's mother was resting at their hotel with the excuse of a migraine, and Keru's father had stayed behind in solidarity. Her mother probably did have a migraine, but it was the kind that came on only when she had to mingle with other families, especially the ones at this luncheon, each stuffed with pride that their child had made it through Yale and was now poised to change the world. Keru couldn't really blame them. She had trouble believing her own hype.

A day later, Keru's parents made a brief appearance at the ceremony, in the back. They smiled hugely but seemed nervous about it and kept their distance from the crowd. Nate's parents missed most of the ceremony because they had gotten lost. They were in the wrong quad and then on the other side of the right one, under an unspecified tree. While Nate was trying to locate them, Keru asked hers if the four of them should meet. Her parents said only if Keru needed them to, otherwise they were okay with not meeting, since they had already met Nate. In the end, no set of parents overlapped, and by the time Nate found his, hers were already half an hour on the road.

The only time their parents would meet was seven years later, at the wedding. They shook hands and congratulated one another on their kids, finally marrying after a long courtship, but they later stood on opposite ends of the room and sat on opposite ends of the dining table.

How Keru's mother had pronounced wedding was *weed-ing*. It was unintentional and her mother could not hear the difference. But maybe there was no difference, Keru thought. Who was the weed, herself or Nate? The weeding of Keru from her family to his, and vice versa. The sudden appearance of a conspicuous foreign plant in an otherwise immaculate lawn.

They had a civil wedding that Keru's parents paid for. Tradition for the bride's family to assume costs, and no one from Nate's side seemed to object. At the wedding, Nate's mother gave a speech and Nate's father gave a speech, and afterward, Nate hugged both of them, while Nate's mother cried. Keru's father gave a speech but not Keru's mother. Her father had never given a wedding speech before and had written nothing down. He didn't mention Nate in his speech, which would go on to upset Nate's parents, who had briefly mentioned Keru. He spoke of his own childhood and siblings, none of whom had passports or visas, so none of whom were present. Keru's father spoke of his late father, a sorghum farmer, who had taught himself how to read and write, and had bestowed on Keru her name. The two characters of her name were *ke* 可 and *ru* 如, strokes Keru's father wrote out midair with his index finger. A direct translation might be to allow or to be in accordance with. The name lacked resolve and sounded soft. To those who spoke Chinese, the name was meant for a girl. "But to those who do not speak Chinese," said Keru's father to the three tables of Nate's family, "Keru is easy enough to pronounce." At this point, Keru's mother was trying to get her husband to sit down and stop talking. But Keru's father held on to the mic and continued. He wished to remind everyone that regardless of what Keru's name means, she was not soft, she was strong. He and his wife had raised their daughter to be strong.

BEFORE NATE'S PARENTS ARRIVED, the bedsheets needed to be washed. Keru wasn't going to do it, so by default, Nate had to do it, and as he started the wash cycle, he said that he felt like a hotel.

"Could be worse," she said. Their parents could be divorced and remarried. Then they would have to contend with four different visits and stepparents. He agreed that that would be worse.

He said he was going to lie down now, and for ten minutes she didn't hear from him, which was peaceful but ultimately kind of lonely. She found him face down on the bed with his clothes on, over the covers that he'd just made. Mantou had curled up beside him, with her chin resting on his back. Keru tried to get their dog to follow her into the living room and sit with her for a change, but Mantou had her favorites, and the order went Nate, Keru's father, Lamb Chop toy, then Keru. Everyone knew the order and commented on it. That she was explicitly at the very bottom made her wonder, ludicrously, if she should get another dog and train it to love her the most. But here were the facts: Keru traveled for work, sometimes five days at a time, and in that period, Mantou probably forgot about her, or assumed she had abandoned the pack. Keru could not, as Nate did, take Mantou to work, have her sit under the desk, and thump her tail against the ground while students dropped by during office hours just to pet their professor's cute dog. Nate wore T-shirts that said THE DOGFATHER. He had a long history of customizing mugs with Mantou's face. As Keru stood at the doorway, promising treats and then literally dangling a bacon-flavored biscuit, Mantou stared back at her in apathy. Eventually Keru returned to the couch with the biscuit.

A dog is not a human child, but that's where her mind went. She could see some version of the following. At first, their human daughter chooses her father, chooses the present parent, the goofball and the one with the softer heart. In adolescence, their daughter taunts Keru for her lack of femininity, her coldness yet lack of coolness, her wrinkles, brown spots, and age, as pubescent daughters are expected to do. Keru could see herself growing resentful of this creature she'd carried around for forty weeks, ballooned into a whale for, and allowed to rip through her vagina. Then there was the fact of race, that the child

47

would be mixed, though Keru could convince herself that race didn't matter. If their daughter chose her father, she would not be choosing to be white or to align with that side of America; her daughter would simply be choosing her father. And if in her mid-to-late twenties, she decides to talk to Keru again—*Tell me about your upbringing, Mom, tell me about China and why didn't you ever take me there, why didn't you ever teach me Chinese, and why didn't we celebrate Chinese holidays, why didn't you teach me to make Chinese food* (so questions charged with blame)—it would have nothing to do with their daughter's desire to be a born-again Asian. No, Keru's biggest fear was the glitch that she'd heard occur among mixed children who were especially rebellious and misguided, armed with a burn-the-house-down mentality. Keru feared that their daughter would become one of those identity-aggrieved people who, in their confused adulthood, went on to renounce their lineage altogether, and to accuse Keru of submitting to the patriarchy, Nate of having an Asian fetish, of which this daughter was the product, a hybrid human, a mongrel child of a fraught yet familiar union.

Nate had listened to each of these dystopias and asked if she had considered the off chance that her child would not reject her. Keru said there was zero chance of that. Some form of rejection for some period of time was inevitable. He shrugged and said, "Okay."

About children, Nate leaned toward not having any. Long ago, he had assumed that to teach at the college level was to be surrounded by adults. This was incorrect. Hundreds of kids went through his classroom each year, and each year a growing subset needed intense one-on-one care. They needed to be assured, during and after class, that they were going to be okay, that science wasn't going to eat them. His older, grumpier colleagues complained about these students, and to fit in he complained alongside them, but secretly he enjoyed being part of his students' support system. He didn't mind holding office hours, extra office hours, and extra, extra office hours. But, given that dealing with kids had become a large part of his job, Nate liked coming home to no kids. None.

Friends with small children offered unsolicited advice.

"You'll change your mind."

"Teaching kids is so different from raising them."

(But how, these friends could not exactly say.)

"Freeze some embryos."

"It's the natural next step."

Their building had several mixed families, and Keru observed one to see what she could expect. She had attempted to befriend the mother, a Shanghai woman, and they were polite when they saw each other, but whenever Keru spoke to her in Chinese, the mother responded in English, so Keru answered in English and that's how it went. Chinese American did not equate with Chinese Chinese. An implicit wall existed between them, invisible to everyone else. Admirable still that despite marrying a white guy, the mother strove to make their children bilingual, though the process looked painful. Whenever Keru saw this family, the father pushed the stroller, saying nothing, while the mother fired rapid Chinese beside it. When the kids replied in English, the mother persisted. *Shuo zhong wen!* Speak Chinese! A chant, like a march, as they crossed the street, went to the playground, waited for buses, got into the elevator, got out of the elevator. Chinese had truly become the children's mother tongue, and Keru could understand their reticence: why speak a language used only by their mother to shout at them, not realizing yet that Chinese is the most shouted language in the world. Once Keru tried Chinese with the daughter. The girl was waiting in the lobby for her parents and doing figure eights on her pink scooter. "I like your scooter," Keru had said, and the girl kept moving in figure eights but her heart-shaped head whipped toward Keru at each turn, her intense black eyes pinned on Keru, her mouth pursed into a pink hyphen. The girl didn't respond in any language, but the suspicion was immediate: Was Keru somehow related to her mother, or was she her mother too? Could there now exist two women forcing her to speak Chinese?

Finally: If they did have kids, she would be forced to change. She more than he. Which didn't seem fair.

"Then we won't have kids," said Nate.

"But hypothetically."

"Then they won't be bilingual."

"But that seems like regression," said Keru. "Two languages down to one. That's like a hundred percent loss."

"Not for me," said Nate.

Nate often hypothesized what would happen to the world if all couples like them stopped procreating. He referenced that movie *Idiocracy*, whose premise is that smart people eventually stop having kids and society descends into ignorance. In the opening scene, a smart couple deems the decision too important to be rushed into, later that it is not the right time. When the time is right, they run into fertility issues, and before they can try in vitro, the man dies of a heart attack while masturbating into a cup. Running in tandem is the story of a dumb couple who lives in the backwoods, surrounded by feral kids. The woman is pregnant again. The man has also impregnated someone else. This family tree grows from children of the actual marriage and its infidelities. The tree of the dumb man has many, many branches, while in the smart couple's tree, only the infertile wife remains.

Nate also liked to reference Darwin. Survival of the fittest is not survival of the strongest or the slyest or the one who can hide best from predators. Reproductive fitness is a numbers game. The female mosquito produces thousands of eggs in her lifetime. A bacterial population doubles every twenty minutes. These were evolutionarily fit species, and after humans were wiped out, they would survive.

"Depressing stuff," said Keru.

"Why?" asked Nate. "You'll be dead by then and so will I."

She forbade him from dying before her. He replied that statistically it was much more likely, by at least six years. "Fuck statistics," she said, and he said, "Yeah, fuck the math of large numbers." Morning dog walks were filled with this kind of talk. Strolls along Central Park West. Promenades around the Great Hill. Other dog parents greeted them and vice versa. They knew the name of every dog on the hill but not of the owners. During good weather, they held hands. In colder months, her hand shrank back into her sleeve and he held on to that sleeve.

THE SHUCKED OYSTER gazed back at her like a rheumy eye. It lay on a bed of ice, alongside its five siblings, in a flower-petal arrangement around a pile of wet lemon wedges. The high school–aged waitress had guaranteed that these were the freshest oysters in Wellfleet and, thus, in all of the Cape. The menu had stated the same, as did the sign outside. Nate's mother insisted on Wellfleet, a town twenty-two miles north of Chatham, for this exact reason. She wanted establishment and a place with at least four hundred Yelp reviews. Fresh meant alive. All six oysters were still alive, and when Keru learned that from the waitress she couldn't bring herself to do what Nate's mother was doing, slurp the living thing down.

No one around them wore masks, and Nate's parents hadn't brought any with them. The strings irritated their ears. His father couldn't breathe under one. His mother worried people wouldn't be able to see her smile. Though restrictions were still in place, his mother didn't care.

"What's the worst they'll do to us, kick us out?" she had said in the car on the drive up, with Keru and Nate in the back seat like two kids after soccer practice. "Deny us entry? We're good, honest folks. We've come all the way here."

Had there been a mask mandate, they might have been asked to leave, but probably not. Nate's mother had a talent, which was endearing herself to strangers. She could place herself in front of the maître d' of a full restaurant, and through chitchat and pleasantries, through a light touch to the arm followed by the admission that she and her husband hailed from North Carolina, west of the mountain ridge, just south of Boone, convince the maître d' of her authentic American humbleness. "Ever been to Boone? You should try to get yourself down there. Go see Grandfather Mountain, Tweetsie Railroad, and the Blowing Rock." Alas, they were a long way from home, weren't they? They were here to visit their son. They'd never been this far north or east before, but since their son refused to visit them (laugh) they'd been forced to visit him. Whoever his mother was trying to win over would be charmed. They would be invited in. Nate found his mother's behavior aggravating, but Keru was amazed. She could not imagine anything like that ever happening to her and her parents. She could not imagine rambling on about Minnesota, or worse, China, and have the maître d' convinced that she was a sane individual to let in.

The restaurant was indeed full, but they were quickly seated on the covered terrace, at a spacious four-top facing the water. The view resembled a striped flag of sand, ocean, and sky. While Keru was staring at this flag, Nate and his father were safeguarding Nate's mother. It was her first time trying oysters, and when given the option to join her, his father had refused, though promised to Heimlich her should the milestone go awry.

"Didn't taste like anything," she said, looking down at the cragged shell in confusion, as if it had been empty all along.

"Put some sauce on it," Nate said.

"Then I would just taste the sauce."

"That's the point," Nate said, and dressed one in cocktail sauce before tipping his head back and sliding it into his mouth.

His mother set the shell down and within a minute managed to sigh twice. "I thought it would taste like something. Faye says it's supposed to taste like the ocean, but what ocean? I didn't even taste salt."

Faye was Nate's aunt, the more well-to-do younger sister who had married an accountant and owned waterfront property off Virginia Beach. She seemed to eat, or at least talk to Nate's mother about eating, oysters all the time.

Nate's mother asked Keru why she wasn't trying any, and Keru lied that her stomach felt funky.

"Funky how?" her mother-in-law asked. "You need a Pepto?"

Keru said she did not.

Nate's father had been waiting on his surf and turf. In a faded T-shirt and cargo shorts, he sat with his chair pushed out from the table to accommodate his spherical gut and his thick left calf that had swung over to rest on his right thigh. Nate's mother was an inch taller than her husband and oscillated in weight, yearly, by thirty pounds. That was like the weight of Keru's leg, and whenever Nate's mother slimmed down, Keru imagined herself hobbling around on one leg. Next to Nate's father, Nate's mother looked overdressed. She wore the same lime-green dress that she'd arrived in and that caused people around her to squint. She was slim again, and told Keru upon arrival that the dress was Lilly Pulitzer and one she had won in a bid on eBay to reward herself for surviving a "mad two-week liquid diet."

"Were you angry?" Keru had asked.

"Why would I be angry?" her mother-in-law replied.

"Like hangry."

"No," she said.

They had been standing in the kitchen while Nate and

his father unloaded the truck bed and Mantou followed Nate around. His parents did not travel light, but instead of coolers of Chinese food, they brought firewood for bonfires, foldable Adirondack chairs to place around these bonfires, liters of Diet Coke and ginger ale, their own coffeemaker, ground beans, and whole milk, for fear that New England stores wouldn't carry their brands. Nate's mother directed where she wanted these items placed and talked more about her dress. While lime green was not her first choice, it was the only color within her budget. Keru asked why the dress had to be Lilly Pulitzer, and his mother seemed hurt that she didn't know who this exciting person was. His mother said the brand was very representative of the area and how could she show up to the Cape without looking the part? Did Keru have any Lilly to wear? If not, they could shop for one together and look like twins.

When his surf and turf came, Nate's father pushed the rest of the oyster platter toward Nate, and to his wife said, "Now you can tell Faye that you've had oysters and it wasn't all that special."

Nate's mother replied curtly that Faye was far more sophisticated than any of them, so Nate's father said that can't be true, since Nate and Keru lived in Manhattan and New Yorkers were, by general consensus, more sophisticated than anyone else. He winked at Nate to disclose that he didn't really think this of New Yorkers, he was just saying it to annoy Nate's mother. Nate's parents

hated coming to Manhattan because they hated its sophisticated traffic. The last time they drove into the city, they
couldn't figure out how to get off the West Side Highway
and ended up somewhere in Jersey, on the verge of a divorce. Nate then had to rent an hourly car and go find
them. "No one knows how to drive," they said of New
Yorkers. "No one knows how to signal or give way."

While Nate and his parents gently ribbed each other
about what was sophisticated and what was not, Keru ordered clam chowder. When it came, the soup had already
turned a pasty yellow and developed an unnatural shine.
To appear like she was doing something, she fished for
gray clam bits with her spoon and then let the bits sink
back down. Nate's parents were really nice to Nate, and at
times it was insufferable how innocuous the conversation
could get. For their first meal together, they were especially delicate with one another. Cheesy jokes about nothing. The winking. Please followed immediately by thank
you, like they had to keep acknowledging one another else
one of them might disappear. Around his parents, Nate
postured. When pressed about it, would say that he didn't,
but he did. He became upbeat, his voice brightened, and
whenever his parents asked about school, in the same
tone an adult might say, *Hey kiddo, how's school going*, Nate
chirped agreeable answers back. Then his father chirped
back a safe retort, next his mother, and Keru wondered if
all white families in public acted like a set of affable birds.

"Who would've thought you liked school so much to

stay for the long haul, huh?" said Nate's dad, and patted his son on the shoulder blade, which he had already done today.

"So true, Dad."

"Nate's always liked school," said his mom. "He loved being read to. He loved *The Phantom Tollbooth*. I keep telling everyone that he taught himself how to read. We played no part in it."

"Thanks, Mom."

"No need to thank us. Thank yourself."

Though she tried, Keru could not always keep up with the stream of pleasantries, and when she forgot a smile or a thank-you, she worried she was perpetuating the stereotype of an uncivilized Asian.

The enormous difference between their mothers had once made Keru laugh audibly. She and Nate were visiting his parents and Nate's mother had dragged up from the basement a large latch box of Nate's childhood drawings. For the next hour, she took out each scribbled sheet, held it between two fingers, and described the image to Keru, while Nate, blushing, left for the kitchen and never returned. After Keru laughed, Nate's mother snapped out of her affable state and said, "You're just jealous your mother isn't more attentive." Many things went through Keru's mind in that instant. Anger. Sadness. The comment was surprisingly mean and honest. Of course Keru was jealous, but it was also more complicated than that and included years of cultural baggage that Nate's mother did not understand. But to have laughed was also mean, so Keru apologized for laughing and Nate's mother thanked her for the apology.

As the waitress cleared their plates, she asked if they wanted anything else. Nate ordered another wheat beer and his mother ordered another wheat beer and Keru ordered another seltzer and Nate's father, who had given up alcohol, another ginger ale. When the drinks came, they clinked their glasses, saying cheers at the same time. Whether Nate's father had truly been an alcoholic, Keru could not say. He used to drink wheat beer, too, and had a can each day like the other dads he resembled. He reminded her of Homer Simpson (who is an alcoholic, Nate reminded her). But five years ago, there had been a frenzy of calls between Nate and his mother. His mother had decided to leave him. Why? Because she believed, no, she knew, saw with her own eyes, that he went to work hungover and drank himself to sleep. He'd been a smoker all through his twenties, had had two heart attacks already, double bypass surgery and a stent.

"The doctor thinks your father's skin is too red," his mother had said.

"Red," Nate repeated.

"Yes, like inflamed."

"And the doctor thinks it's from the drinking."

"Well, the doctor doesn't know, but what I think is

that your father can't control himself. I found beer in the garage."

"He always keeps beer in the garage."

"But at his age? And the doctor's right, his skin has never been this red before. He looks like an Indian."

Said over speakerphone while Nate was folding laundry in their bedroom and Keru happened to be in the same room, applying lotion. Keru stiffened and looked at Nate, who quickly took the phone off speaker and then hung up.

At the time of the inflamed skin comment, Keru had been a daughter-in-law for three years. The *in-law* gave her a comfortable sense of distance, but she would have preferred the word *daughter* be left out, as in the Chinese system, where she would simply be called wife of son. All mothers wish to feel needed, but Keru found that her mother-in-law really yearned to feel needed and especially to be heard. After Nate left for college, she experienced severe empty-nest syndrome but couldn't admit that to herself or say the words *empty nest* aloud. She called her sister more, sent Ethan envelopes of money. She asked Nate's grandmother to move out of her nursing home and in with them. The grandmother declined. So Nate's mother turned her full attention to Nate's father and looked for signs that he was in trouble, which he may very well have been, though he had not increased his weekly intake of beers and Nate could not remember his father ever showing up to work drunk or hungover. "Oh, but he has," said his mother. "Lots of times. Countless. He just hides it from you and me and us." So, without question, Nate's father would have to listen to her and stop killing himself through recreational alcohol use, else she would leave him.

"Has she thought of what would happen postdivorce? Like, where would she go?" Keru had asked when this was happening.

"Mom doesn't think," Nate said. "She feels."

Now two wheat beers in and his mother was visibly tipsy. She was wiping her nose a lot and touching her cheeks with the back of her hand. The mention of *The Phantom Tollbooth* stirred something in her, and she fell into one of these feeling patterns and began naming all the things Nate had once loved. He loved Boy Scouts, camping, Scholastic Book Fairs, pencil erasers, board games, *Wheel of Fortune*, rubber cement, coconut cookies, Ghostbusters anything, foosball, air hockey, darts, percussion instruments, spelling bees, chemistry sets, furry animals, scaly animals, magic tricks, running, walking, and sitting.

When his mother finished, Keru said, "What a great inventory of things to have loved." She probably could have done without the "have loved." She probably should have just nodded.

The table went silent as it usually did when wife of son said something out of sync and hard to interpret. An awkward minute later, Nate's father flagged the waitress down for the check.

On the last morning of her own visit, Keru's mother had tried to give Keru some advice.

"Don't be snarky."

"Don't irritate his mother."

"Don't say what you're thinking."

"Don't talk politics."

"I don't talk politics with them," Keru said, though that was a fat lie.

Her mother smacked the kitchen counter and Keru jumped. "Let it go, okay? Who cares what they believe in? They raised Nate to be a good person. He's very good and loyal to you. Give them some credit for that."

Keru promised to give credit where credit was due, and to conduct herself in a way that did not suggest she'd been raised by wolves or former communists. That Keru's family had once been part of the Party was information Nate asked her not to disclose to his parents. "Nate," Keru said very carefully. "Everyone in that country commits to the Party in some form or another. That's what a one-party system means." Besides, she agreed with her mother that Nate had been raised well and was well loved, but increasingly these factors paled against the challenge of pleasing her in-laws, two individuals of the undisputable largest generation, boomers born at the end of McCarthyism, who had lived through and contributed to a long period of dominance and supposed greatness to which half the country wished to return. This was the complication Keru had failed to consider until she gained such in-laws, and realized, oh fuck, so that's what's meant by the phrase you marry the family.

But had he married her family?

Did he have any idea who they were?

Did she? She knew her parents were both born in 1960, the second year of the Great Famine. Six years later, Chairman Mao launched the Cultural Revolution, which lasted another ten years. Schools closed and her mother's relatives, all teachers, were sent away for reeducation in rural areas. About this period, her mother had remained evasive. Food was being rationed and those not sent away stood in long lines for milk, millet, and rice. The lucky few received meat. Her mother lived with a neighbor and played with other orphaned kids in the building. Her official stance: "There was chaos, yes, but it was not the blight the West likes to make it out to be." Then one day, everyone returned, thinner but reeducated. Her mother moved back in with her family, resumed school, and life went on. Keru's father was even more evasive. The revolution went fine for him and his family, he'd insisted, since they were already impoverished and lived in the rural fields where reeducation took place. After the revolution, her father managed to test into university, a one in two hundred chance at the time. "How?" Keru would ask. "I studied." "But how?" "With my brain." At university, he met Keru's mother. "But how did you meet? Who introduced you? What did your families think of the match?" There were large differences in class, education, manners, and dialect. City people versus the country bumpkins. "And whose idea was it to leave the country, and how did your families feel about that?" Details her parents never elaborated on. We met, married, had you. We live here now. The end. That her parents had decided to shutter off a large amount of their history was perplexing, even hurtful. But was this a way to protect her? A coping mechanism or a show of strength? Was this standard Chinese taciturnity or something else?

NATE'S MOTHER had asked to see lighthouses and came with a list of five notable ones along the shore. She had perused multiple sources and home magazines to create her list, based on which lighthouse grabbed her attention the most. His mother made lists all the time, especially for holiday meals and road trips. At first, Keru thought the habit reflected an organized mind, but Nate said it more accurately reflected a scattered one. The five lighthouses were not along the same route. Two east of Chatham, and three very far north, one at the very tip of the peninsula, in Provincetown, yet she wished to see all five on the same day, else the trip would feel incomplete.

"How about two today and the rest tomorrow?" Nate suggested, scanning the list. It was the next morning, and they'd just finished breakfast. Keru was standing by the sink, loading the dishwasher as slowly as possible, so she could be somewhere in the room but not involved in the conversation.

His mother didn't like the idea of splitting the lighthouses. Tomorrow, she'd intended to go to the beach and really sit on the beach and read. "You don't read," said Nate, and his mother said, "But I could." Did Nate know (he did) that Aunt Faye followed celebrity book clubs and, supposedly, read a book a week, then sent Nate's mother these books to read? Now she had a tower of books in her house that she didn't know what to do with. Most were either too current or too preachy. "I don't want overly complicated," Nate's mother had said, scrunching her nose at the word *complicated.* "I don't want characters I can't understand. What's wrong with Danielle Steel?" And did Nate forget (he had) that the day after tomorrow was the weekly farmers market? They needed to buy fresh seafood, lobsters, clams, corn on the cob, summer sausage, local cheeses, and watermelon for their afternoon barbecue and bonfire.

"Then we can't do this entire list," said Nate.

"I'm sure we can."

"We can't."

"You're being dramatic."

Nate tossed the notebook page back at her and said firmly, "No, we can't." He was not driving for half the day just for her to see her five lighthouses when there was already one nearby.

"Who said you had to drive? Your father can drive."

"The truck's uncomfortable," said Nate.

"You'll live," said his mother.

"I won't, actually," said Nate. "I won't live, Mom."

"He's being dramatic," she said to Nate's father, who sat on the couch, silent, watching a football game with a pint of ginger ale on his stomach.

Nate proposed separate cars.

His mother wanted them to be in the same car.

"Not enough space," said Nate, who insisted on bringing Mantou, since when they had gone to Wellfleet for oysters, they had to leave the whimpering dog behind.

"Mandy can sit on someone's lap," his mother said. They didn't want to butcher the pronunciation, so they called the dog something else entirely.

"Absolutely not," Nate said.

"Why not?" his mother asked. "When was the last time all of us sat in the same car? When was the last time all of us had a chance to talk?"

Nate said they were talking right now.

This went on for twenty more minutes.

After which, Nate, Keru, and his parents drove, in separate cars, to Chatham Lighthouse. Fifty feet tall, it had everything his mother had asked for—a white tower, cast-iron railings, a station with a red roof. She said the overall effect was okay, but it wasn't on her list. They walked along the perimeter. Keru had Mantou on leash, but it was still hard to control her when she was in a new place, excited, and pulling ahead like a horse. Nate played tour guide, read through the series of plaques about the history of the lighthouse and encouraged his parents to read them as well. His father glanced at a few and grunted. Then he found a bench to sit on where he could repeatedly clean his sunglasses, adjust his baseball cap, and look askance. He had trouble with parking again and had met them at the lighthouse ten minutes later, after first dropping Nate's mother off. He said he didn't understand why parking was always such a pain in these areas, why it was only street parking and only for thirty minutes.

"How's anyone supposed to see anything?" he asked. What if they had wanted to picnic?

On leash, Mantou was choking herself and making a scene. By pulling her back, Keru looked like an animal abuser, or at the very least an unfit dog owner. Nate's dad asked Keru why she didn't just let her off.

"All dogs have to be leashed," said Keru.

Her father-in-law said it's not like Mandy would hurt anyone.

"I think we would get in trouble," Keru said.

"Yeah, so what. What's the worst they could do?"

Keru wondered why her in-laws were like this, why they valued noncompliance only when it suited them. She said there were fines.

Her father-in-law rolled his eyes and said, "Well, sheesh."

Nate's mother walked behind Nate and read, or pretended to, all the plaques. She was also sweating profusely and dabbing her forehead with a paper napkin. She waved at Nate's father and pointed to the empty space beside her where he was supposed to stand. Her husband waved back.

Soon, Keru was pulled by Mantou away from her white family toward a large group of tourists huddled at the base of the lighthouse tower, taking selfies with peace signs. These were direct-from-Asia tourists, possibly Korea, by the way that they were double masked, wore wide-brim canvas hats, long sleeves, long pants, and still carried an umbrella (the women) or had a towel draped over their shoulders (the men). No one in that group would risk catching the virus or being darkened by the freewheeling American sun. When Mantou got too close, the women shrank back, while the men came forward and gestured for Keru to keep her distance.

Eventually Keru had enough of people and sat down on an empty square of green lawn. She made Mantou sit too. She texted her mother a picture of the lighthouse. Her mother didn't reply to the picture, but it showed on Keru's phone that the text had been read. Her parents had arrived back in Minnesota safely, having driven back the same as they had left, in straight shifts, and eating trail mix in their car.

The tourist group resumed their selfies and eventually moved on to couple shots. Some couples matched in outfits, down to the color of their canvas hats, and seeing them pose together, Keru wondered something she wondered often, should she have married someone more like herself? Her junior high and high schools were predominately white, and though she had crushes on a few people, no one had a crush on her. College was quite different, the East Coast, the Ivies, and suddenly she was surrounded by smart, eligible men. During her first two years at Yale, she had joined every Asian group and taken the premed sequence of classes. She had planned on becoming a doctor, but that desire slipped away when she realized she was blood averse, disease averse, and that her premed classmates would eventually become her colleagues. She and this premed, Peter, from microbiology went on a few dates. She learned a lot about Peter. He was a National Merit presidential something or other, as was she, and had been named one of the top ten U.S. high schoolers to watch by *USA Today*, which she had not. Peter had no questions for her. After he ran out of things to say, he went back to reading and would only lift his narrow head from his thick textbook to correct her Chinese if she were on the phone with her mother. As Keru was breaking up with him, he remained largely unimpressed. He said he knew she would do this, having predicted her actions and even her breakup speech from the start, no surprises there. "Your head is too tapered," she replied. "Probably because someone you pissed off slammed it between two books." Once medicine was out, she took microeconomics, and in a class that was over 50 percent Asian, she met Shang. Shang was more talkative than Peter, though he could only talk money, which shouldn't have surprised her, but somehow still did. He planned on graduating summa cum laude in Econ, then moving from one investment firm to another until he made managing director. He knew the salary he needed to start on. He knew how much this number would need to increase each year. Shang did at least ask what she was interested in. She said undecided, but definitely neither medicine nor finance. He suggested consulting, a decent way to make bank while you figured out your path. A consultant saw different industries, traveled, and had generous expense accounts. Solid advice, until Shang added that more girls went into consulting since it was by and large easier than finance. At restaurants, Shang never tipped above 15 percent. He would ask for the receipt and scrutinize each line on their cab ride home. The cab ride she would cover, their explicit date night arrangement. Shang was also a virgin and needed to have sex with her as soon as possible. He made her sit on his dorm bed and watch violent bank heist movies that put her in no mood for sex. During the credits, he would kiss her with his wet, droopy eyes clenched shut, like he was having a nightmare. A month of many heists but no sex led Shang to sleep with another Asian girl from their Econ class without telling Keru or taking the time to dump her. He just pretended Keru didn't exist anymore, and when she passed him again in class, Shang would have a neck spasm and become fascinated with the ceiling. Not long after that, the president of the school's Taiwanese association asked her out. It was 5 a.m., and they were postering campus kiosks for their annual night market that gave students a chance to try at least twelve different types of dumplings. James was two years older, tall, fit, had lush, thick hair that he regularly flipped back and forth. Keru lost her virginity to him, and a full committed semester in, met his parents. They shared hot pot at a local Sichuan restaurant, and Keru thought everything was going great, that this was it, her big Yale love story, until after a summer of sporadic contact and no sex (because James was in Taiwan), James sat her down in a crowded D-hall and relayed that his mother didn't want him to be with someone from the mainland. "The mainland," Keru repeated. "Taiwan is its own country," James said, to which Keru agreed but asked what did geopolitics have to do with them? Keru left when she was six. The mainland didn't want her anymore nor did she feel much kinship toward it these days. James said that while he fully understood her perspective, he also didn't want their future kids to have to choose between two heritages, and being fully Taiwanese himself, he was glad he didn't have to. Keru reminded him that he was also American, as she was, and he said, "Yeah, but *Taiwanese* American, and you're *Chinese* American." Since then, Keru had always been uneasy around this need to differentiate, down to the modifier, among the Asian community, a community that, while not monolithic, also lacked unity. But resisting the urge to explode in a D-hall, she asked why this specific concern hadn't come up earlier, like during week one. He'd known she was from China, and for the rest of her life, this fact could not be changed. James nodded sympathetically. For what it was worth, he assured her that he had loved her, but this affection, which once seemed exponential, had plateaued, and as he thought more about his future, taken an asymptotic turn down. With his hand, James pantomimed a nose dive. Keru watched his hand hit the wood dining table like a plane dropping out of the sky. She said she took it back. She didn't think Taiwan was its own country after all.

For a year, she stopped thinking about boys entirely. Her mother asked if she was gay, and she answered, "So what if I am, what's my sexual orientation to you?" No, of course Keru didn't say that, she didn't want to die. She said, instead, that she was focusing on her studies and applying to consulting jobs. But alone in her single, she looked down at her dingy underwear, at her unshaven legs, at the small fold of fat developing above her dingy underwear band from meals of solely mozzarella sticks. So, for her last college Halloween, she dressed herself in whatever she could find and asked the first person she saw in the dorm where she could party. There were parties on every floor, this person told her, slumped against a banister, already drunk. She went down a random hall, through a random open door, and into a random room that had loud music, a large crowd, and a guy in the corner strapped to a homemade shark fin, dancing poorly by himself. There were better-looking men at this party, better dancers. But she kept looking over at the friendless guy who had no clue he was being watched. To approach was a risk, because what if he was alone for a reason, what if he was a demented frat boy with a fetish. If he was a demented frat boy with a fetish, she would have to fight him to the death. Before she approached, she made a mental algorithm of what she would do, when and how she could make her escape, should she need to, and what objects in the vicinity she could throw.

A month later, they declared themselves official and shared their first impressions of each other.

"You were ready to fight me?" he asked.

"Only if you were a bad person."

He seemed disturbed by that and could only look down at his hands.

"But you're not a bad person," she clarified.

"I just thought you were cute," he said.

Keru had been called many things, but cute was usually not one of them. Objectively she was. Small and cute, and when sitting with her knees pressed into her chest, she took up very little space.

"Oh," she said, surprised. "I see."

KERU SAT next to her mother-in-law, in their respective beachwear, on a beach that her mother-in-law had chosen, named the area's most quintessential family beach, so here they all were. Keru wore a black one-piece that showed no cleavage or waist or desire to be in a swimsuit. Her mother-in-law wore a colorful one-shoulder number with wide compression bands in the midsection that made one look cinched in, sculpted, but didn't allow one to do anything else, like swim. The two women shared a towel while the men went to see about the food trucks that had lined up along the entrance. Keru felt like a displaced wax doll in an anthropological exhibit labeled MODERN HOMO SAPIENS ON HOLIDAY: starved females await the males' return from an arduous chorizo taco hunt; starved females must occupy themselves.

The sun was very bright and there were kids at this beach, at least a hundred of them, screaming their tiny lungs out and trying to kill one another with plastic buckets and sand.

Her mother-in-law had been holding a one-sided discussion about children, how adorable they were from one age group to the next. She would find a child on the beach and point to them, then describe to Keru what Nate was like at that age, then move on to a slightly older child.

"You and Nate would make good parents," she had said. "Nate would be such a great dad."

Keru had said "Hmm."

"All parents want to become grandparents."

Keru didn't have a response. She was sort of frozen, feeling as if her body were not hers to control. Because it wasn't. She had tasks, according to those around her. To carry on the gene pool, to fend off idiocracy, to birth the first of her lineage in America, to give their four parents new hope, to ensure Nate a chance to be a good dad.

When her mother-in-law's arm rubbed against her own, Keru shivered.

"I hope you know how much we love you," she said, their arms now stuck together from sweat, sunscreen, and whatever else.

"Yes," Keru said, shivering.

"Both of you. We love you very much, and we hope you'll come down to see us more. At least twice a year."

Keru said she loved them too.

The saying you loved each other business was much like the thanks one. You had to remind the other person regularly, else they forgot. Nate was the first to tell Keru that he loved her, and now they said it to each other every day, which she enjoyed, because she did, in fact, love her husband, and it was nice to know, explicitly, that he loved her too. Keru also loved her parents, but that was a different kind of love, and they didn't address it aloud. With her in-laws, Keru cared to the extent that she was supposed to. She wanted them to be happy and healthy, she wanted good things for them like financial stability in their old age, but she didn't think she loved them, nor did she believe they truly loved her.

"Kids will expand your capacity to love," said her mother-in-law. "Kids will make you feel more present."

Keru hated this kind of romanticism, but what could she say against it? Her mother-in-law was a mother and she was not.

"The first is usually harder," her mother-in-law continued. "Ethan would throw these tantrums. Go stiff as a board and not want to be touched. In public he would lay on the ground and pound it, then if you tried to pry him up, he would grab on to anything. The handle of a door, a pole, your hair. I thought something was wrong with him," she said.

Something *is* wrong with him, Keru believed.

"Nate was entirely different. The most docile baby. Quiet and happy, always smiling. Ethan and Nate were very sweet to each other," she said. "They're in a phase right now, but they'll get over it. Siblings have a bond that can't be explained."

This kind of romanticism Keru didn't mind, for she'd always wanted a sibling. As long as she could remember. A brother, a sister, anyone would do. She asked when they'd last seen Ethan.

"He calls," their mother said. "More than Nate does, at least." She stopped to take a big breath, and then said, "I've realized that Nate and I aren't as close as we used to be. Do you know why?"

Keru thought everyone knew why, but instead of saying that, she said, "Nate always plans to call, but forgets. It's improved, hasn't it? And we're here now, so."

Her mother-in-law glanced at her sideways. There was sun in her eyes and sand on her cheeks. "Maybe it has and maybe it hasn't. You know him better now, as it probably should be."

Strange to hear her mother-in-law say that. Strange because it was accurate and self-aware. Had they broken new ground? Were they now supposed to hold hands? As if also discomfited by the moment, Nate's mother stood up and said she was going into the water.

"Be careful," Keru said.

"Will do," his mother said.

The why was that Nate had ideals, and when those close to him let him down, he had trouble forgiving them for their faults. In 2016, his parents had made clear who they stood behind and so had he. Nate was never much into politics, but as that year progressed, he followed the news too closely and made statements to Keru like, "I'm looking up at a huge wave about to crush me and everything I believe." This was entirely hyperbolic, no wave was coming for him, and regardless of who won on November 8th, he would go to work the next day, come home, cook, eat, shower, sleep, have sex, pay taxes, walk the dog. In the grand scheme of daily life, nothing would change. But on election night, neither of them had slept thanks to noise in the streets, unrest, and someone screaming for hours, from a rooftop, "THEY LET HIM INTO THE WHITE HOUSE THEY LET HIM INTO THE WHITE HOUSE." Then on November 9th, his mother sent the group chat a happy face emoji and a message saying that now all that nonsense was over, they could finally relax and enjoy the holidays. Train tickets had already been bought, vacation days requested, and a thirty-pound turkey waited in their basement freezer when, upon seeing that tiny, pin-sized emoji, Nate called his mom to say that he wasn't coming back for Thanksgiving or Christmas (and hadn't been home since).

He asked his mother why she had sent that emoji to the group chat, which included Keru. For the obvious reason that she was happy, his mother said. He explained that he was not happy. He was not happy at all. "I'm sorry you feel that way," she said. "But I should be allowed to express myself. This is my country too." About not coming home, his mother thought he was bluffing.

"You're being dramatic," she said.

"I'm upset. There's a difference."

"You're willing to do this to your own mother? You're willing to ruin this holiday for me forever? Do you even have a heart?"

"Ethan doesn't come back."

"Ethan can't help himself."

Nate said his decision was final.

His mother started to cry, so the phone was passed to his father, who, in a voice of gravitas, said all the sad fatherly things. "I don't even know who you are anymore. You should know better than to upset your mother. You've let us down. I can't say I stand by your decision. I definitely don't understand it. When you've come to your senses, call us, we love you, and we love Keru."

Keru thought this immediately: after crying and venting to her husband, Nate's mother would hang her son's Thanksgiving cancellation over politics on his new Asian wife, who might be far more sensitive to these things and, perhaps in retaliation for some immigrant woes she and her family had experienced, sought to infiltrate the stronghold of American values by taking their Nate.

"Do you think she thinks that I poisoned his mind?" Keru asked a white friend.

"Yes," this funny friend said. "A hundred percent. But she'll say you're the exception, which you are. You haven't poisoned my mind yet."

Unwisely, Keru sought the advice of her mother, who dismissed Nate's estrangement as an impulsive act of a young person. "Young people lack perspective," her mother said. "They don't know how to suffer. At most, whoever they elect is in office for eight years. What's that compared to an entire childhood spent under Chairman Mao?"

There was no avoiding the Mao card.

Like there was no avoiding the Trump card.

Keru's parents did not vote nor would they. They were indifferent to who won and, on the whole, to democracy. But her mother told Keru that Nate and his family had to care about the politics, because it was their politics. She told Keru to protect herself, she need not get involved. Stay neutral and out of it. Then, ironically, she ordered Keru to fix the situation by calling Nate's mother and having a brief but direct talk. "Apologize if you have to."

"Apologize for what? She's his mother."

"Then remind him of that."

"I think he knows."

The term passed, and they survived. They survived another election cycle, a global pandemic, both sides steadfast in their beliefs.

Keru watched her mother-in-law wade into the water and lower her entire body under, such that just her head was visible. Her head bobbed up and down as she moved cautiously in a small circle, away from a group of reckless teens. Waiflike tan girls mounted themselves on the backs of strong tan boys. The boys rammed one another, the girls squealed. Teenage Keru would never have fit in here. She and her parents would never have come to this beach and had they by mistake, they would have sat in a corner, away from everyone else. Apologize for what? Keru knew.

A shadow came over her. Physical, not metaphoric.

"Where's that giant dog of yours?" said the shadow, and without making out its features, Keru remembered the voice.

"Excuse me?" Keru said.

"Your enormous dog."

"I don't understand."

But Keru did understand. The shadow belonged to the woman Keru had thrown a rock at and missed. Had the rock hit its mark, the woman would likely not be here. She would be gone. But alas this woman was standing over her, alive, well, and wet, having just been in the ocean, and now dripping salt water on Keru's dry towel. Her swimsuit was similar to that of her mother-in-law. Same diagonal stripe across the torso, same compression system in the middle to give bulging abdomens the hint of a waist.

"You tried to kill me the other day," said the woman, with anger.

"Pardon?" Keru said.

The woman repeated her sentence about Keru being a killer.

"You. With a rock," she added. "You're a psychopath. I'm here to tell you that, you psychopath."

But Keru feigned more incomprehension. She gazed out at the ocean instead of up at that leathery, pink face. The woman came a little closer and put one foot on the towel, in case the towel ran away. She accused Keru of more unpleasantness, and in a low voice said that Keru was in serious need of psychiatric help.

Keru asked the woman to speak a little louder. She thought if she was being accused of so many things, at least let this be publicly known.

"You heard me," said the woman.

"Not sure I did," said Keru.

"You definitely heard."

"Unfortunately not," said Keru.

The woman made Keru nervous, but it also seemed unlikely that her swimsuit could conceal a gun. The worst case was that the woman would lunge at her and try to strangle her in front of a PG-13 crowd. Keru could outlunge her. She could fall over left or right, and by the powers of momentum, the woman would trip over herself and dive into the sand. The woman didn't lunge, but also didn't move. She had her hands on her stomach for a while, glaring down at Keru, deciding what she could do. Finally, she leaned in close to Keru's face, right up to her ear, which Keru couldn't pull away else it would show fear. Keru worried about being spit on, or in a creepy turn of events, licked, but the woman only whispered, "Leave, you shouldn't be here, go," and then smiled at Keru like she had really landed a zinger, like Keru had never heard anything worse. Keru had heard much worse, had also from a distance been spat on. But that didn't mean she looked forward to hearing the woman's comment or, in trying to forget about it, committing it to memory. That was the problem with these comments. Keru remembered them all.

"Hey, who are you?" shouted a voice from behind the woman. "What did you just say to her?"

The woman turned around to take in Nate's mother, whose face was crimson from having run out of the water.

The two women were of the same height and build. Had they linked arms, they could have cancanned in sync.

"This girl tried to kill me," the woman said, pointing down at Keru. "I'm going to report her."

"Don't think so," said Nate's mother, swatting at the air in front of the woman, then standing between her and Keru. "Wrong person. Please go away. Leave my daughter alone."

The woman made an effort to look unfazed while trying to make sense of the new information. She scratched her loose and leathery neck. Keru too was confused, until she realized that she was the daughter.

"Leave us alone," said Nate's mother. "Or I'll report you." Then she reached into her beach bag and took out her phone. Holding the phone upside down, with the screen locked, she threatened that if the woman refused to leave, she was going to take her picture and send it straight to 911. Could you send photos to 911? Keru wondered. Would someone at 911 see the pictures and dislike them on your behalf?

The woman stepped off their towel quickly, even though the phone was clearly upside down and no one was taking a photo of anyone. When the woman was far enough away, Nate's mother dropped the phone and sat down with a thud. Her forehead was scrunched and she, too, seemed perplexed at what she had done.

"You okay?" she asked.

Keru said, "I'm okay."

"What a kook," she said.

Keru said, "Yeah, what a kook."

Once Nate and his father returned with a tray full of tacos, Nate's mother relayed the incident in urgent detail. The men were quiet, sitting around the towel, checking in on the tacos but not eating them.

"Out of nowhere, this woman just appeared," she said, fanning her fingers out in dramatic fashion. "I could tell something wasn't right about her. Something was off about her body language. She said Keru tried to kill her. Total nutcase. All this stuff you hear in the news about Asians getting harassed, and your father and I keep thinking, would anything like that ever happen to Keru? Is Nate looking out for her enough? Had I not been there, she probably would've gotten physical. She came this close to Keru's face." Her mother-in-law demonstrated. "The woman was literally breathing on her."

When her mother-in-law drew close, Keru held her breath. When the demonstration was over, she exhaled. Nate's mother asked Keru what the woman had said to her.

"Nothing worth mentioning," said Keru, who just wanted the whole ordeal to be over so everyone could eat a taco.

"But she did say something to you," insisted Nate's mother. "I saw her say something to you. Was it very racist?"

Keru said she couldn't remember.

"You'll let us know, won't you?"

Keru said once she remembered the racist thing the woman said, she would be sure to let everyone know.

ON THE DRIVE BACK (they had taken one car to the beach, the truck), Nate's mother continued to express disbelief about the incident. She called it an "incident" and used air quotes for unknown reasons. Had anyone seen this woman lurking about their rental compound or stalking Keru before? No one had. Keru considered telling Nate's mother about the rock, but would then have had to answer more questions, all of which seemed tedious, like why she threw a rock in the first place, did she have a habit of throwing things, did she have undisclosed anger issues, could she take control of these issues and not throw things in the future?

"I should have taken her picture," Nate's mother said. "I should have found someone right after or followed the woman to show we weren't to be messed with. You mess with one of us, you mess with all. We have to complain."

"Complain to who?" asked Nate.

"The beach, the people who manage that beach, they can't be allowing crazies in. Children play there. It's meant to be a safe place."

Nate asked for the situation to be left alone.

"I can't," said his mother. "It ruined our day."

At the cottage, Keru changed, showered, and hid in the bedroom. From bed, she texted her mother scenic pictures of waves and verbose messages about how they were having a fun-filled, collaborative time. She texted Nate in short blocks. She wasn't coming out for dinner. She wasn't hungry. Her current plan was to pass out and sleep it off, wake up a new person. Nate replied with a thumbs-up.

The "incident" had happened to Keru; it was her day that had been ruined.

On the bright side, at least the woman hadn't been very racist. She hadn't pulled back the corners of her eyes or called Keru a chink. Go back to your shithole country, chink, stop ruining ours, that would have been very racist; everything else fell short.

A long time ago, Keru had arrived at the conclusion that she and her parents had been tricked. Her father was never promoted despite an impeccable work record. Her mother tried to work but found it easier to make no money and be extremely frugal. The friends of her parents were all Chinese immigrants, and whenever they gathered, they gathered inside, never outside where they might be stared at, inside where they could speak Chinese and feel safe. Stay neutral and out of it. Protect yourself. Find your shield. But how was this life better? An ability to endure hardship had, in America, been translated into a willingness to accept less. Yet here was the bizarre contradiction, here was Stockholm syndrome at play. While Keru's parents could never assimilate, there was a chance that their daughter could. So Keru felt two forces, the push of her parents to assimilate and the pull of the fabled white family who, worst-case scenario, sends you off to bed without meatloaf and you stomp upstairs to an ongoing laugh track, and later your mother comes to give you chocolates and your forehead a good-night kiss. The dream of a family that skis and surfs together, leaves cookies out for Santa, strums acoustic guitars around a campfire, folds foreigners into its ranks willingly, and has endearing dysfunctions but never real ones. This family did not exist, or maybe Keru had chosen poorly. A sample size problem: she had married into one white family, not every.

But had Nate's mother redeemed herself? Could her actions at the beach be considered gallant? If not gallant, decent? By stepping in, Nate's mother had been incredibly decent, and Keru was grateful to her mother-in-law, a good white person, for having saved her from a bad one. Though Keru had not asked to be saved, nor was she incapable of saving herself. The dream of the white mother was problematic. The dream of the white knight was also problematic. So what if your white mother became your white knight? Was this like two wrongs made a right?

Inside Keru's mind lived a large Möbius strip that looped at high speeds.

Outside, she could hear talking, the television clicking on, an announcer's voice, stadium applause, Mantou barking, the whoosh of a thrown ball, gallops and the full mass of a panda dog slamming into the bedroom door, to complete the fetch.

THE NEXT DAY, Keru had coffee with Nate's family but wanted to skip the farmers market to catch up on work. Nate's mother cooed for Keru to reconsider and came close enough to stroke Keru's hair.

"I have work," said Keru, moving out of hair-stroking range. "I'll walk Mantou."

Once everyone else left, Mantou slumped by the door and stared at her. The expression wasn't neutral and said, explicitly, "Mom, the rest of our pack has abandoned us because you're such a loser."

When Keru opened her laptop and loaded her inbox, hundreds of emails filed in, most with deadlines in red and words like "Actionable Item Number 1." She thought about replying to an email. She thought about hitting delete all. Then she closed the laptop, got the leash, and took her afflicted dog outside. Mantou pulled and bit the leash, but Keru did not let her off. They circled the rental property, then strolled to the beach but stayed along the edge. In a 360-degree manner, Keru triple-checked her surroundings for crazy people who might look sane. But how sane did she look, swinging her head left, right, back, then back again. She passed numerous ALL DOGS MUST BE LEASHED signs, at least one on every post and way more than she had noticed before. One sign seemed to offer a different message, so she stopped to read it. The message was: Whoever's daughter you are, you're not one of us. Pilgrims used to thrive here, the true settlers of America. European immigrants, Caucasian immigrants, blue-blood Americans (and the Obamas). Even your panda dog doesn't belong here for he's only half white. But the sign couldn't have said this because the sign didn't have text. It was simply a black silhouette of a big dog trapped in a red circle, bearing a red slash.

THERE WAS A PROPER WAY to lay firewood in the fire pit to achieve maximum flame. Nate had learned from his father who had learned from his father who had learned, if Keru had to guess, from Paul Bunyan himself. In the minimal backyard, on an open dirt patch, with a shallow sink hole, Nate and his father started laying down logs, diagonally, then crisscross, then upward like the spokes of a teepee. When everything was ready, his father took out some tinder, lit it with the grill lighter, and cupped the small fireball in his hands, blowing gently at it through his fingers before setting it in the middle of the logs. They called to Nate's mother, who was inside, when the tinder caught and they had fire. They hooted in jubilation, raising all of their arms.

A few hours earlier, Nate had taken a shower, and Keru, not wishing to be alone with her in-laws, had sat in the bathroom with him, on the toilet. Mantou was curled up around the toilet as well. They were crammed in there, Keru's feet on top of their dog's back. She told Nate that she wanted to go home. "Two more days," he said from behind the curtain. "And then we can go home." She said she wanted a drink. He said that could be arranged. The message was passed on, and as the men built fires and the women prepared dinner, his mother took a can of hard seltzer out from the fridge, clicked it open with her fingernail, and placed it in front of Keru.

"You can drink, you know," she said. "His dad and I won't mind. Please drink, we bought a six-pack. We have beer and wine too. Whatever you want."

Keru felt like a psych patient being told to take her meds. She brought the can to her lips, drank a quarter of it in one go.

They ate around the fire with plastic utensils. The Adirondack chairs were enormous, and it was a squeeze to fit four around the fire without two knocking up against the screen door.

"Next time we should rent a property with a bigger outdoor space," Nate's mother said. Driving around, she'd seen places with swimming pools, large stone decks, pizza ovens, a proper fire pit with dedicated chairs. "Wouldn't that be nice?"

"That would be nice," said Nate.

"Super nice," said Keru.

Keru wanted to like her mother-in-law and for this woman to like her, but they seemed prone to misinterpret each other. For example, this request for nicer accommodations, which Keru had looked into last winter and found swimming pool rentals out of their price range. Her own parents had offered to contribute, money that Keru had refused, since the stay itself was a gift. Her in-laws hadn't offered to contribute because they couldn't have and Keru was fine with that as well.

But to request something better was then to assume that someone else can pay.

Nate's parents found explicit money talk disagreeable. From credit card debt to retirement plans, nothing was ever revealed, and it was unclear if his parents could retire. Nate's best guess was no, not without Social Security and downsizing their house. "So what are they going to do?" Keru asked. Nate was cavalier about the issue and said "probably nothing." It was his parents' problem, not theirs. Curious though, the nature of families, how one person's problem can often become the problem of another. Years ago, Nate had proposed and Keru had accepted, but prior to giving his blessing, her father asked his daughter if Nate had any debts. To not incur debt, the immigrant Chinese family saves. To save, they live well below their means, which are already meager. There are years of no presents, vacations, or cable, no trips to the hair salon or even that cheap place at the mall (because your mother cuts your hair, cuts your father's hair, and your father cuts your mother's hair in the basement of their almost paid-off house). This family becomes debt-free at high cost. They are assiduous and proud. So to oblige her proud father, Keru asked Nate the uneasy debt question. In response he looked dazed, blew out a puff of air, and thought hard. The exact amount, he wasn't sure of, but somewhere close to sixty thousand for a loan he took out in college. Sixty wasn't zero, but it also wasn't a million, so Keru contacted Nate's mother, who had co-signed the loan. Nate's mother looked for these loan papers, which had not been stored in a clearly labeled latch box as had Nate's drawings. The loan papers were misplaced, "lost," said Nate's mother, so Keru called the loan agency and spoke to a real person who directed her to a repayment portal that neither Nate nor his parents knew about.

When Keru finally logged into the portal, she saw a number that caused her to refresh the page. The grace period had long ended, after which the interest rate had quadrupled, and now ten years out of undergrad, the amount had become much larger than before. "Did you know?" she asked Nate. He provided a soft nonanswer that boiled down to everyone has debt. This country is run on debt. Forgiveness will come. Hakuna matata. About the now much larger sum, her father threw a fit. "You are not to marry into this family until they have paid off every cent of that debt themselves. You are not to marry a man with debt. We are not here to bail them out." From there Keru had three options. She and Nate could break up or elope, or she could use her own savings, the entirety of it, to pay off his loan in full.

The day the balance came to zero, she printed out the confirmation page, stuffed it in a drawer, and told her father it was taken care of, without going into details. "His parents came through, didn't they?" he concluded, for Keru's father did not believe in the existence of an entrenched white family without money, and Keru had given up convincing him otherwise.

"They must be hiding it from you and Nate," he would say, "they must not want Nate to have it, for the eldest's sake." Without explicitly saying so, her father still envisioned Nate belonging to a dynastic family, of trust funds, offshore assets, and convoluted wills, who were purposely discreet with their finances around Keru because she was Chinese.

Tired of this nonsense, Keru once had to say, "Dad, there are poor white people in this country, you know." "Maybe a few," her dad replied, "but not many." How else to explain their rich hay baling neighbor, a man richer than any farmer her father had ever known. China had nine hundred million farmers; none drove the cars that this neighbor drove. So Keru gave up. Let her father believe what he wished.

When Nate learned what his wife had done, he was grateful but also perturbed by a gesture that he deemed wholly unnecessary, since either he would have paid it off or hakuna matata.

When Nate's mother learned what Keru had done, she sent Keru a private text, thanking her for the good deed, with the inclusion, "and please thank, I suspect, your father, for helping our Nathan as well."

That text convinced Keru that the cultural gulf between their parents was too wide. They could be locked in the same room forever and never understand one another. Yet the knowledge of how Nate's loan was paid for allowed Nate's mother to assume that Keru and her family were much more well off and could afford things like, theoretically, a larger rental property with a swimming pool or even a vacation home for all of them to use in the future.

The fire had been growing taller and started to send smoke into their eyes constantly. For Nate and his parents, it devolved into a game, which way the smoke would go and which person had to duck and shut their eyes. For Keru, it was nonsensical. They could have gone inside, like Mantou, where there was air-conditioning, no insects, and no smoke. They could have not lit the fire.

Nate's mother was particularly loquacious this evening and seemed to draw energy from the flame. She spoke about people back in their town, Nate's old neighbors, teachers, and schoolmates, and how often she was asked for Nate updates, since it seemed that out of all of them, the boy would go far. She asked if Nate had heard from Ethan recently. Nate shook his head.

"I wish you two were closer," she said. "Brothers are meant to help each other. You guys should figure it out."

"Not much to figure out," said Nate.

"He's family, Nathan. Blood. You can't call him once in a while to check in?"

"I don't want to check in, that's not my job."

"No, guess not," his mother said. She flicked a gnat off her shirt. There were gnats everywhere and the smoke seemed to have made them delirious. Nate's father moved his plastic fork around his plastic plate, poorly separating his grilled meat pieces from his vegetables. Keru put a whole slice of zucchini in her mouth and let it sit there, dissolving, while she looked straight ahead at the space between Nate and his mother, but not directly at either. She watched the fire dance and a swarm of drunk gnats lift up toward the roof of the house like a dirty balloon.

"Then whose job is it?" his mother asked. "You never call me or your dad. We never talk unless I reach out. At least Ethan tries to stay in touch."

"Because he's using you, Mom. He only reaches out when he wants something. He only says things you want to hear."

"I don't feel used," she said. She turned to Nate's father and asked if he felt used, and he didn't move his head very decidedly in any direction. He asked why they had to talk about any of this now.

"We're all here," his mother said.

"That's no reason," his father said.

"I need a reason?" his mother asked.

The zucchini in Keru's mouth had liquified and been swallowed. She considered eating another one but felt self-conscious about moving.

"You should have been a lawyer," his mother said to Nate, casually but also flatly. There was no warmth around the remark. "You're eloquent, well read. You did debate team, Model UN, aced Honors Civics. Ethan gets himself into messes without realizing it, and a lawyer in the family could have really helped."

"He realizes it," said Nate.

"He doesn't have a clue," said his mother.

"Ethan knows exactly what he gets himself into each time he gets into it," said Nate.

"You and Ethan are much alike," said his mother.

"So you tell me," said Nate.

"But what he lacks is patience, foresight, and a determination to do the right thing, all traits we saw in you a long, long time ago," said Nate's mother. "When we tell people what you're doing now, people who know you, they're always surprised. We say so are we. Your father and I had always assumed you'd make a better lawyer than scientist."

"I like science," said Nate.

"I'm not saying you don't, but law might have suited you better. You would have fit in more."

Nate told his mother she's said enough, and his mother replied, "What I'm saying is that we've visited you in lab. We've seen who works in them, all those grad students and postdocs."

"Mom."

"Let's face it, you're a minority there. You're up against some very accomplished people and you have to work harder than you need to, to stand out. Certain groups are better at science and math. They like to work themselves to death."

"Mom."

"What?"

"Please stop talking."

"I'm just telling you what we've observed. What we saw."

"And I'm telling you to shut up."

Nate's father attempted to get up but only managed to lean forward. "That's not how we talk to one another in this family," he said. He asked Nate to apologize.

Nate said no.

"Then we sit here until you do."

"He doesn't need to apologize," said Nate's mother. "He just needs to think about what I said."

With that, Keru realized what she disliked about her mother-in-law. The woman demanded to be understood by everyone around her, yet was not willing, ready, or able to extend the generosity to others.

"I think I'm going inside," Keru said, standing and brushing ash off her clothes.

Nate's mother glanced up, surprised, and said, "What? No, stay. I'm not talking about you, Keru. I was trying to get Nate to see that he didn't pick an easy route."

"Which route is that?" Keru asked, not going inside.

"Your father, for example," she said, looking and pointing at Keru, though Keru was less than two feet away. "A very smart man. Knows a lot about fuel cells. Took the hard route, the only route. But if Nate has to compete with someone like that, he really needs to know what he's doing. He has to be even better, and sometimes we worry."

"Worry about what?" Keru asked.

"That it's overwhelming," said Nate's father.

"Tiring," said Nate's mother.

"Unhealthy."

"Impossible."

"A little unfair."

Nate's face was twitching but not forming words. Keru sensed that he was trapped in his own Möbius strip: *Is it my place to speak or can my wife handle this tricky issue herself? Was this issue actually about race, or did it only appear to be? If my wife did react, would she be overreacting? Should I pray? Or jump straight in the fire?*

"I hope anyone with a job knows what they're doing in that job," Keru said. "I hope people are not just failing upward or asking for more than they deserve."

"That's not what I mean," his mother snapped.

"It's not?"

"This is coming out all wrong. You and your family have done well for yourselves, and we're lucky to have you. I'm not trying to say otherwise."

"Then what are you trying to say?" asked Keru, who wished to give Nate's mother the chance to be as clear as possible, so there would be no more misunderstandings.

His mother paused to consider her words. Eventually she said, "We love you, Keru, and we hope that you love us too. But just as you wouldn't want us to change you, we wouldn't want you to change us. We're different, but that doesn't mean we can't coexist."

"Coexist," said Keru.

"Exactly," said his mother.

"But not turn you guys into me or my parents," said Keru. "Not dilute you in any way or turn Nate into a chink."

Nate's mother sucked her mouth back into her face. Nate stared down at the ground.

"I don't like that word," said Nate's father, shaking his head. "And we don't use it here. We've never used that word."

"You're right," Keru said. "It's a very racist word." A word that Keru can even remember learning. There was the racist version and the version used in phrases like the chinking of bracelets or a chink in the armor. How had she parsed out the difference? How had her parents learned the word? (The racist version, they didn't know about the other one.) Grade school. Seatmates. "Are you a chink?" this seatmate asks. He'd heard the word somewhere, most likely his family, siblings, or parents. "I don't know," the girl says. "Are you?" The seatmate doesn't think so. Then the girl goes home and tells her parents and the parents say it means nothing, but don't talk to that boy again, focus on your studies. To that aim, the girl gets her hands on a dictionary and looks the word up.

"Keru, you've put us in an uncomfortable situation," her father-in-law said. "So I want to assure you that we're not saying what you think we're saying, and whatever it is that you think about us is untrue."

Keru sensed she was being scolded in the tone of pseudo-reason and patience. The meaning was, Hey look, you said it, not us. We're the good guys.

For three seconds there was silence, and Nate's mother asked if anyone wanted fruit. On the plastic foldout table was a halved seedless watermelon. Beside it a large knife to cut off slices.

"I could do with some watermelon," said Nate's father, pleased with this outcome.

"Nate? Keru?" Nate's mother asked.

Nate said nothing. His mother emphasized that the watermelon was seedless.

"Sure, I'll have some," said Keru, because eating fruit after a meal was important.

"All righty then," his mother said, a swing in her voice like the music was back on. She rose to cut the watermelon. Nate's father rose to tend to the fire.

"You think we need another log?" he asked Nate, who could not make eye contact with him.

"Don't think so, Dad," he said. "Think we should just go inside."

"Another log it is," his father said, and from the pile behind him pulled out a large one that wasn't like the others. This log was taller, thicker, and had some faded red and blue paint on it, some stars-and-stripes patterning. "Fourth of July décor," his father explained, a complete non sequitur. "Your mom wants to get rid of it. Been in our basement for years."

The log merely sat there, not catching except along the edges, and stifling the fire that already was. Nate tapped Keru on the knee and said he was going inside; did she want to come? It was a polite ask. He was telling her, not asking. But Keru didn't want to go inside anymore. She was already outside, waiting for her watermelon, and if they went inside now, they would forfeit enjoying the rest of the evening, which was still, weatherwise, very fine. Nate stood up to go in. This won't do, Keru thought. Together is better. Together we suffer. On the ground beside the woodpile was the hatchet that Nate's father had brought to split more wood. Keru picked the hatchet up, its metal handle weighty and cold. The log's stars and stripes were staring at her and perhaps testing her. It was a dumb patriotic pillar, not a flag.

Still, she thought, something like that shouldn't be burned.

So, she thought, I shan't let it burn.

The hatchet dug into the cracked wood, and with a firm grip on the handle, Keru hoisted the flaming thing out of the fire and threw it, along with the hatchet, into the house. The pillar crashed through the screen door, into the kitchen, and lay on the tile floor, radiating smoke. The dog leapt off the couch and tried to attack it. Someone screamed. It wasn't Keru. Someone pushed past her, ran through the screen door, breaking the frame off completely, and doused the log with a water pitcher. Doused it again. When the smoke cleared, three people stood in the kitchen scrutinizing the wet piece of burnt wood and the black streaks it had left. One by one, they turned their wax heads to Keru, through this new doorless opening, achieved by collective effort. Why were they looking at her like that? Why the confusion? The fear? She, for one, had neither. Her head was perfectly clear. At least now they could get back to that seedless watermelon and the task of coexistence. At least the pillar had been saved by her, Paul Bunyan reincarnate, with an axe. A fire alarm flashed and blared somewhere. The

large security deposit she'd paid was gone. A one-star re-
view awaited her upon checkout. Blame me, she thought.
I'm the bad one. In the meantime, she sat back down by
the fire and beckoned for her chosen family to come out
and join her.

INTERLUDE

We move Nate and Keru forward five years. Their parents they see periodically but never for more than two days at a time, never back-to-back, and never on the Cape. Keru and her in-laws are civil, meaning she only talks to them when she has to, like when Nate receives tenure. The day this happens, he is taken to dinner by his colleagues and fed glass after glass of brown liquor. "Did you tell your parents?" Keru asks, and he, happily tipsy, says no. When she calls with the news, Nate's father answers. "I see," his father says. "Good on him." That's the last conversation Keru has with her father-in-law before he has his third heart attack, this time fatal.

Here is the last conversation Nate has with him: His father is already experiencing chest pains when he calls his son. "Might be a heart attack," he says, while driving himself to the hospital. "But should be fine. They'll get me fixed up. Talk soon." He faints at the hospital, in a flimsy, backless gown, with Nate's mother still on her way, driving below the speed limit, thinking it's just like the first two times.

Six months after Nate's father dies, Keru's mother, a born-again hypochondriac, begins what she calls her medical years. During a routine endoscopy, she receives a cancer diagnosis, which becomes a cancer misdiagnosis, after which she slips on an ice cube in her own house and fractures her ankle in several places. Bedridden, her foot in a cast, she calls Keru with hyperbolic concerns, like will she ever be able to walk again (yes), will they amputate the foot (no).

At her consulting firm, Keru makes partner and her income doubles. Even taking inflation into account, Nate's post-tenure income stays relatively the same. Whenever Nate calls attention to this discrepancy, Keru purses her mouth and thinks of the myriad things she could say, but should not.

An eight-month post opens up in Chicago, a rare opportunity for Keru to prove that she can run, as a new partner, the Midwest division. Chicago is also closer to her parents. She and Nate discuss the separation, the eight months apart. With no kids, they are supposed to be flexible. So to Chicago Keru goes, and from there, every other week, to her parents' house to sit with her mother. Her father, retired, sometimes sits with them, too, but prefers to garden, so excuses himself to do more of that.

Keru returns to New York whenever she can for a long weekend, during which time she, Nate, and Mantou do nothing, because she's tired, and he's tired, and being tired all the time is tiring. But a two-week holiday is imminent, and Nate asks if they should attempt to do something over nothing. Keru is indifferent, and Nate says he is, too, but in truth, is not. He wants to get away somewhere, just them and their dog. A second honeymoon of sorts, to unplug and reconnect.

"What does Mantou think?" she asks Nate over FaceTime, while she's with her mother (asleep) and he's in their living room with Mantou. Nate pans the phone to their dog, who has been pacing around the coffee table without reason, pacing just to pace. While the vets call Mantou, at nine, a senior dog, Nate and Keru do not.

Rubin's vase is that well-known optical illusion. Does one see a vase or the profiles of two people, face-to-face? Taken further, is the vase empty or full? Say the individuals are a couple. If they're silent, they're bored. But when they converse, they disagree. Full, one person says about the vase (the optimist). Empty, says the other (the pessimist).

There is a tendency to take two halves of something and assign them equal weight. Marriage is fifty-fifty, but who said that? Who believes this to be true?

PART TWO

oliage is the mass dying of deciduous leaves. To witness this death, hordes of people drive northward and eastward to places like the Catskills. The many towns in the Catskills are called hamlets. A hamlet is a town within a town, a village of sorts, that has its own post office but no government or well-defined borders. The word comes from the old French *ham*, which is equivalent to the old English *hām*, which is equivalent to the modern English *home*. A hamlet can have decent landscape, tall mountains, large lakes, etc. It can have lots of houses, not all of them homes. Home is not a given and, for many, a hard, sometimes impossible place to find.

TWO HOURS north of the city is a hamlet with a lake. Nate chose this area but left the other details up to Keru. She was less picky about the location, more so with accommodations. "We could go to the Hamptons," she'd suggested—same etymology as the word *hamlet*—and as usual, he'd replied, "Ugh, the Hamptons," so they never did.

Driving, Nate saw silver slivers of the lake through tree trunks. He asked if they should stop to take in the views, and Keru said they had two weeks to take in the views. She would rather get to the bungalow, unpack, and shower. Mantou had laid down in the back seat. The dog was carsick, and they'd stopped several times already for her to saunter off to a corner and throw up.

Last month, Nate had turned forty, and to celebrate, Keru had flown back from Chicago on a weeknight. "Something low key," he'd requested. "No party, just the two of us," and they'd gone out, just the two of them, to one of those upscale restaurants that only served bite-size portions on comically large plates. The dinner and service were excellent, but he kept buttoning and unbuttoning his dinner jacket. A dinner jacket was required. He would not have been allowed in otherwise.

"The average life span is seventy-seven," he'd said during their second-to-last course of caviar served over a foam of bonito broth.

"I see where you're going with this," she said, taking pictures of the foam that she would show no one.

He'd proposed that they go camping.

Keru said that at middle age, she preferred to sleep inside.

So when his wife booked the bungalow, he had been

elated. He'd assumed a simple cabin or a log hut. They would have a quaint but poorly maintained backyard of yellow grass. They could make a pitcher of sweet tea and hang out on their uneven porch, under the shade of a hundred-year-old tree. His grandfather had lived and died in a bungalow. His grandfather also kept his washing machine in his front yard. Nate looked forward to going as far off-grid as possible. He hoped that their nearest neighbor was at least a few minutes' drive away.

Then they arrived at their intended location, and an imposing matte black gate. The gate required a code that Keru knew, and as they drove through, Nate confronted a clearing of ten pristine miniature mansions, all connected by clean sidewalks and small gathering pavilions equipped with shiny aluminum grills and cushioned, new-looking Adirondack chairs. Each bungalow had white paneling, flower beds, and a porch swing adorned with gingham pillows. Not a speck of dirt was out of place.

Keru listed the amenities. A twenty-four-hour concierge. Discreet housekeeping. Grounds, immaculately maintained. Ultra-high-speed wi-fi.

He told Keru that this was not what he expected. He tried his best to sound casual.

"We're on vacation," she said.

"Yeah, but do we need all this?"

She stepped on the gas to swerve into the parking lot. "No one *needs* to go on vacation, Nate. We could all just work until we die."

Of course, Keru was quoting his mother, and of course, Nate never knew how to respond.

The one-bed bungalow had a modern kitchen, a sitting area, and a sleek metal deck with glass railings that overlooked the lake. The lake was surrounded by prime foliage, the kind they'd come to see. Impossible, Nate thought, since this view was supposed to be elsewhere, hidden by trees and accessible only from designated lookout points that required reaching a summit. Now it was his turn to quote his mother-in-law: Where's the suffering? Show me the suffering. But they'd taken some turns to get here, gone a long stretch uphill, maybe even tunneled through a luxury wormhole. While Nate was out on this deck, piecing together their navigation, Keru put their food bags in the kitchen, their suitcase in the bedroom, and their bathroom kits in the en suite with the clawfoot soaking tub. The moment she set Mantou's memory foam bed down, their dog curled into it and, possibly, sighed. Keru leaned in to feel her nose. She told Nate that the nose was still dry, and he came over to feel the nose as well. They placed fresh water in front of her, which she ignored. They dabbed water droplets on her dry nose, which she hated. Why their dog had become sullen, no one knew. Vet 1 thought hormonal. Vet 2 neurological. When blood tests returned normal, vet 3 suggested a second dog, a puppy sibling. During that visit, Keru had been in Chicago, so only Nate was physically in the exam room with their dog and his wife on video. "I'm not sure we can commit to that right now," she said. "Anything else we can try?" Vet 3 prescribed antianxiety meds and antinausea meds, the same as vets 1 and 2.

Keru had separated the anxiety and nausea pills into their own labeled capsules. They, along with the specialty kibble for dogs with sensitive stomachs, had already been set upright on the kitchen island with notes written by Keru to herself. Nate knew what to feed their dog and when because these were his tasks, but "notes couldn't hurt," said Keru, should he forget. As his more organized and efficient wife showered, Nate attempted to unpack their suitcase. The attempt was thwarted by color-coordinated packing cubes, each containing some subset of their garments, in some unknown arrangement that he didn't want to mess up, so he closed the suitcase and left it to Keru.

Cooking was still Nate's domain, and for dinner he brined and baked chicken in a casserole pan, made rice on the stovetop. Keru's only job was to open the wine, and once she did, they ate on the deck, quietly, with their sullen, medicated dog under the table.

The meal became so quiet that Nate said he wouldn't have minded a place without wi-fi.

"You're welcome to not use the internet," she said.

"You know that's not what I mean."

"The chicken is very tender," she said.

WEIKE WANG

"What I mean is that I can't decide if I like it here," he said.

"I think you want to like it here," she said.

"I want to, yes."

"Then like it."

But Nate worried what staying in a gated vacation complex said about the people they'd become. He told her if this was what she wanted, they might as well have gone to the Hamptons.

"I really don't know what you have against the Hamptons," she said.

"Oh, come on," he said.

"Because how can you have something against a place you've never been? What have the Hamptons ever done to you?"

He hated when his wife argued against him for the sake of argument. She smiled, knowing that she had won.

"We're comfortable," she said.

"Which, while not a pressing, immediate problem, could have repercussions up ahead," he replied.

"You want us to be less comfortable?" she asked.

"No," he said after a long pause.

THE CHILD HID behind his mother and pulled on her dress. The mother swatted at him, told him to explore the bungalow or to go sit on the porch swing. The father carried a booster seat and set it on the steps before petting the child's head, thus messing up the child's hair. This was the family that had rented the bungalow next door and to whom Nate waved the next morning from the communal pavilion, where he was investigating how to use the grill. Eventually the father came over to shake Nate's hand. Up close, he was short, small, and looked in his early thirties at most.

"Good morning neighbor," he said. A booming voice. "We're from the city. Brooklyn. Park Slope. Zip code 11217." An assertive Eastern European accent. "Where are you from?"

Nate said Manhattan.

"Ah, okay. Where in Manhattan? We like Manhattan."

"The Upper West Side. Zip code 10024."

"Yes, we know that area. We have been there many, many times for brunch."

Nate had his opinions about brunch and the Upper West Side. They'd lived in the hundreds before, but for a better condo rental had moved down. Zip code 10024 was what he'd expected. Too nice, too comfortable, with too many cafés, restaurants, and his simple opinion about brunch was that it was just lunch.

The father pointed to himself, then behind him to each person in his family. His name was Mircea, hers was Elena, their son's was Lucian.

"Like Mircea the Elder," Mircea said, and Nate nodded, though he had no idea who that was.

Mircea called Elena over—"Come, meet our neighbor"—

and immediately Elena did, while Lucian sat perfectly still on the cushioned porch swing of their bungalow.

"You came here alone, then," Mircea said, with no indication that he was asking a question, but he waited for an answer. It took Nate a moment to realize this and then to explain. Alone? No. His wife was inside. Their dog.

"Perfect," said Elena. A soft voice. A milder accent. A round, cherubic face, framed by wavy, auburn hair. But she was taller and larger than Mircea, who stood with a slumped back, thin hands in his pocket. "Luka loves dogs," she said. "We have a dog but could not bring him to the States. He's with my mother. We miss our dog."

It was a bright, sunny day, and as Nate started to say goodbye, Mircea said, "Let's have coffee. Call your wife out and we'll have coffee together here, in thirty minutes. We'll bring the coffee. You bring your dog."

Nate said that he had no problem with coffee, but didn't think his wife would be up for it. "She's more of a homebody," he said, and Mircea smiled, one jagged front tooth, in an otherwise aligned set, as if he didn't believe in the existence of that word.

Inside, Nate told Keru about the neighbors and their impromptu request. He said, "Isn't that odd," and she asked why hadn't he agreed.

"We're not here to meet people," he said dismissively. "At least not in a serious way."

"Coffee isn't serious," said Keru, already changing out

of her lounge pants into outdoor clothes. "What else do we have to do?"

"Make our own coffee."

"We can do that tomorrow."

Twenty minutes later, Nate was sitting next to Mircea around an unlit fire pit with a cup of strong coffee. Elena had come out with a large French press and four mugs. Mircea had brought a wood tray with saucers of olive oil and a sliced baguette.

"It's fresh," he'd said to Keru, handing her a piece. "Try. We passed a boulangerie on the way here. See, still warm. The beans and oil we bought in Brooklyn. There's a shop around the corner that imports their oils from Catalonia. We like oils from there more than, say, Andalucía. The beans are roasted in small batches."

"That's very generous of you," said Keru, taking the piece with her free hand and holding the coffee in the other. She looked from one hand to another, unable to decide which to try first.

The morning was cool enough that Nate could see the steam coming off the coffees and everyone's breath. Mantou was sniffing the lawn of another bungalow, with Lucian a few steps behind, trying to catch her nine-inch tail. Whenever Mantou went, Lucian followed and was batted in the face by the tail, but seemed to enjoy it. Mantou was also of the right size that Lucian kept asking his mother if he could ride him. Elena translated the boy's request, and after Keru said no and Nate said no, she told the boy no and in stern English, "You must be gentle."

Luka was six, just starting school. Elena explained that in the home they spoke Romanian, but English out. The boy understood some English, went to an English-speaking school for five hours a day and had after-school activities.

"Don't forget the birthday parties," said Mircea. They went to at least one a week.

"He'll be fluent before we go back," said Elena, as she soaked her bread pieces in the oil from Catalonia and not Andalucía.

"Hopefully," said Mircea.

"There is not a doubt in my mind," said Elena.

"Back to Romania?" asked Keru.

"No, Rotterdam," she said. "Where Luka was born."

"So, you're from Rotterdam," asked Keru.

"No, we're from Romania," said Mircea, with a quick follow-up: Where was Keru from?

To Nate's surprise, his wife said China instead of what she usually said, like the city or the Midwest.

"Yes, that part is clear," said Mircea, leaning over the fire pit and closer to Keru. "But where in China?"

She named the province and Mircea said, "But where in that province?"

She named the town, and Mircea said that while he hadn't been there, he'd been to Changsha for a conference.

Years ago, prepandemic and pre-Luka. Elena came along, and they'd toured Zhangjiajie and Fenghuang.

"Am I saying it right?" asked Mircea, and Keru said that remarkably he was.

"The people," said Mircea.

"Very warm, very welcoming," said Elena.

"The scenery," said Elena.

"Unforgettable," said Mircea.

"And we thought Europe was old," said Elena.

"But you guys are older," finished her husband.

It finally came out that Mircea was an economist, though when he told them, he winced and added, "Macro is my job, not who I am." He had a two-year post at the Fed, after which they would return to Rotterdam.

Nate asked what the Fed was like.

"Lots of Italians," said Mircea. A guffaw followed by a head toss.

Keru asked Elena if she was at the Fed too.

"Oh, that's not for me," said Elena, with a shudder. "Numbers, markets. Certainly not. For now, I take care of Luka and the house. Then once we go back, we'll see."

"Elena's an artist," said Mircea. "She paints, sketches. She has a studio."

"In the city?" asked Keru.

"No, upstairs," said Elena. The top floor of their townhouse was her studio. It had the best light.

At the word *townhouse*, Nate glanced at Keru, who

seemed amused. They were still in a two-bed, though more spacious and in a building with a doorman.

"The townhouse is too large," said Elena, scrunching her nose. "It is literally a house that's also a town. Beautiful but altogether far too large."

"Yes," said Mircea, as solemn about this inconvenience as his wife. The residence was provided through his work so they had no choice in the matter except to live in a large and beautiful house.

"Half the time I'm on one floor looking for something that's on another," said Elena, nose still scrunched. "Though that is the only problem. Everything else is perfect."

AFTER COFFEE, Mircea and Elena said they would need to go inside and "have a nap." Then they would "have a hike" around the lake. When Mircea invited them to join, Keru said "yeah, maybe," and Nate made this unnecessary joke, "Join what, the nap or the hike?"

Mircea scratched his chin and said, "Of course I mean the hike."

"Oh, that wasn't—" said Nate.

"He's terrible at jokes," said Elena.

"I am," Mircea admitted, head lowered.

"So don't bother," said Elena.

"She's right," he said, head still down.

Alone in their bungalow, Keru asked Nate why he had to make that joke.

"Why?" he asked back. Then having no answer, he asked why she had to overanalyze it.

"I don't want them to think we're weird."

He didn't think the joke was that weird.

"It was awkward."

He didn't think it was that awkward. He was being obstinate on purpose. So, she pivoted.

"I wish we were more like that," she said.

"Like what?"

"But I don't think we ever were."

"Like what?" he asked, distressed.

"They make everything look so easy," she said.

He didn't think they made anything look easy. Who could have an easy life in a monstrous townhouse with an attic art studio? How much anguish that family must go through for the sake of art.

"I'm trying to tell you something," she said.

As was he.

"I was never like that in my thirties," she said. "Or twenties. I make everything look hard."

"You're still in your thirties." He reminded her.

But by year's end, she would be forty, and he imagined she had some feelings about it, none that she had explicitly expressed, except that she didn't want a party or their friends to make a big deal of it or a day filled with fanfare.

To make her feel better, he said that career-wise their thirties were meant to be hard, and that he didn't miss that decade, though he did miss waking up without migraines. She went to the other side of the living room to tidy up the throw pillows that he'd thrown off the couch earlier to make more room for his legs.

"Should we see them again?" she asked from that side of the room, and from this side of the room, he said, "Only if you want to."

"It could make our time here more fun," she said, piling the pillows back on.

He asked if hanging out with strangers was something she considered fun.

"They're not strangers anymore," she said.

"People we barely know."

"Then what do you want to do?" she asked, karate chopping a V into a pillow. "What's on Nate's fun plan for the day?"

He said why they couldn't just stay indoors, cook, and do their own thing. Why pay all this money to stay at this ridiculous compound if not to at least enjoy the space and each other's company?

"Unless you don't think my company is enough," he said offhandedly, as if this were not his deep-seated concern.

"Amazing that you keep calling it a compound," she said.

"But that's what it is."

"A compound makes it sound like jail."

"Does it feel like jail?"

She ignored his comment and sat down among all her karate-chopped pillows to read a book. The book did well to cover her face.

"That doesn't look comfortable," he told her.

"Who needs to be comfortable in jail."

He did some imperceptible eye rolling. "We could stroll down to the lake."

She said she was currently more interested in her book.

While Keru read for the next hour, Nate sat with his phone. The internet was truly high speed, and that nothing lagged for even a millisecond soon began to bother him. After doom scrolling through the headlines, he decided a better use of his time was to shut himself in the bedroom and call his mother. He made the effort each week, and each week they had the same conversation. Perfunctory updates. Discussions about current and future weather patterns. His mother was in remarkable health. No high cholesterol, hypertension, or dental problems, no heart attacks.

When he described their accommodations, his mother was also confused. "How can a bungalow be fancy? That's an oxymoron." She asked if all the oxymoron bungalows were filled. He said most weren't.

"Because who can afford it," she said. "The economy is tanking."

"It's not, actually."

"Not for you guys."

"Right, okay."

"A nice thing would have been to invite Ethan."

"Ethan?"

"The son I had before you."

"Oh, that guy."

She told him that Ethan was "doing good" again. He'd found landscaping work at some prep school, in one of those nice areas of Connecticut. "Found a lady friend already, of course," and while these temporary girlfriends used to bother their mother, she was glad now that Ethan had company.

"You should've invited him and the lady friend to your bungalow," she said.

"That's an option." He had no intention of inviting anyone. But he told his mother that they weren't alone, they had Elena and Mircea, fine, reliable neighbors who napped, hiked, and insisted on having coffee.

"What kind of name is Mirka?" his mother asked.

"Mircea. It's Romanian."

"They flew all the way from Romania to the Catskills?"

"No, they're from Park Slope temporarily but actually from Rotterdam."

"Where's that?"

"Brooklyn."

"Rotterdam is in Brooklyn?"

"Rotterdam is in the Netherlands. Park Slope is in Brooklyn."

His mother was quiet. Then she said, "I find that very confusing."

"Not really," he said. "Not if you just think about it."

"A person should come from one place. I don't understand why some people need to come from more."

His mother asked if Mircea's wife was also from Romania or Park Slope or Rotterdam.

He said yeah.

His mother asked if Mircea's wife was Asian.

He said no.

"But these are just neighbors, not friends."

"Correct."

His mother sighed, and Nate knew what she was thinking. They'd had a version of this conversation many times before. "You used to have lots of friends, Nathan. What happened to all of them? You had friends in every grade." Nate wasn't in school anymore, except as a professor. "Parents have friends," was his mother's other line of argument. "When kids go to school together, you naturally make new friends. Dad-groups. Mom-groups. It's all very organic." When Nate asked where all her parent-friends were, she said, "They moved away." A few years back, it had finally dawned on her that he and Keru weren't having kids and that had sent her into a deep depression. "I guess I will never be a grandma," she'd said. "I guess you're dead set on denying me that chance." His mother's sister was already a grandmother thrice over, and his mother had never imagined that she would be permanently behind. "When Faye sends me pictures of her grandbabies, what am I supposed to show her?" Nate suggested the tulip garden or pictures of her two cats. His mother called him facetious and asked, "Who are you going to talk to when you're my age? Who are you going to call?" Facetiously, Nate said, "No one," which aggravated his mother further and caused her to rant. "Most adults on this planet are parents, and to understand most adults and your own parents, you must become parents. Else you will never understand anything, Nathan. You will be completely oblivious to everything that's good." She then railed against the liberals and how their cynicism for traditional family values was destroying society, like aphids destroyed plants. "Kids are the future," she said. "An objective truth, not an optimistic one," Nate replied. "The world isn't all bad," she said, and Nate asked if she had had kids for the world. "Well, no," she started to say, but then informed him that this was beside the point, he was missing the point, the big picture, the grand scheme of things, and no good came from his acting this way.

When Keru took the Chicago post, his mother had assumed that they were on the brink of divorce. Something must have prompted the move; something must have changed.

"You would tell me if she was leaving you?"

"You would tell me if she ran off with someone?

"You would tell me if she got pregnant and didn't want the child?"

"No, I probably wouldn't have," he said to the abortion question. That was his limit. But he'd explained that Chicago was a good opportunity and placed Keru closer to her parents, who were aging. His mother said she was aging at the same rate and asked why Keru was allowed to be closer to her parents but not him. He said he would move closer if he could (a lie). But why did Keru need to work at all after he'd been tenured, his mother pressed, why couldn't she stay on part time and have kids, she pressed and pressed, until one day, he said, quite plainly, that they could live on her income but not the reverse. His mother seemed shocked by this, and Nate tried to defend himself. Industry has always paid more, but academia offered prestige, ideals, a chance to chase knowledge for knowledge's sake and pass that knowledge on. "Prestige," said his mother, in a manner so ridden with doubt that Nate filled in the rest. You can't live off prestige, can you? You can't physically scoop it out of the jar like caviar and feed yourself with it, and you certainly can't afford rent, food, leisure activities, or save enough for retirement in the most expensive city in America without a spouse who also works and ideally makes more. Not that his mother would ever belittle him, but when he mentioned the high cost of living, rising inflation, she did say, "No one forced you guys to live in that city. No one made you stay in school."

From the bungalow bedroom, he said he would talk to her later. She said they'd hadn't been talking that long to begin with.

He said he was going to hang up now, which caused her

to ask, "What's gotten into you lately" and whether he was seeing a therapist.

A pause for both sides to collect themselves and remember that they were two adults without therapists.

"Oh Nathan, don't be so down on yourself," she said in a tone that filled him with woe. "I felt inferior to your father for years. I was perpetually in his shadow. But at the end of the day, remember that you're your own person and that you do great work too."

He regretted telling his mother too much and not enough. Either was a betrayal, and always he was stuck in the middle. But he did feel inferior to Keru and could not admit this so frankly to anyone. To anyone except his mother, he would sound at best like a man-child and at worst like a misogynist. He hoped he wasn't a misogynist, but the possibility couldn't be ruled out completely, so at his annual physical, Nate told his PCP that sometimes, without cause, he got nervous and produced more palm sweat than usual and had trouble falling and staying asleep. "I worry I'm just puttering around," he couldn't bring himself to say. "I worry nothing I do really matters." Within ten minutes, the doctor had diagnosed Nate with anxiety and written him a script for Xanax that Nate never filled. The doctor found nothing abnormal with Nate's vitals or blood panel, but suggested that his patient exercise more, and to sleep better, completely exhaust himself before bed.

"I'm already completely exhausted before bed," Nate said. "I just lie there thinking."

"Yeah?" said his doctor, with his back to Nate, typing at his computer. "And what exactly are we thinking about?"

"Nothing of value," said Nate. "Just noise, dread. Like I'm hurtling toward some great disaster."

His doctor kept typing. "And by great disaster, we mean?"

"Death, mortality, nothingness."

His doctor noted these down.

That night, at home, Nate made himself a salad. While washing and dressing the lettuce, he thought about death—his father's and eventually his own—and overwhelmed by inevitability, he overdressed the salad and had to wash the leaves again. On the day of his father's funeral he'd been exceedingly anxious. Anxious about his mother, his brother, about his wife being in the same vicinity as his other relatives, who knew about Keru but had never met her. Before setting the funeral date, he'd called his brother six times and left five voice messages. "Seems short notice," Ethan said on the sixth call, and had concerns over the high price of airfare, of gas, and that he was currently between jobs. Nate paid for Ethan to be there. Then, once Ethan arrived, their mother wrote him a check from their father's life insurance. At the service itself, he and Ethan each said a paragraph. Their mother read from the Bible. Their paternal aunts were late. As his mother read through Scripture, she took dramatic pauses to look up, over her reading glasses, at the family. He could feel her speaking to him. "It's just you and me now, Nathan. Don't let me down."

ON THEIR WEBSITE, the alpaca farm forbade dogs, and after reading the policies, Nate called to confirm. "Not even well-behaved dogs on leash?" The woman said no and directed him to the same page that Nate had just read. "It'll only be a few hours," Keru said, and had set up in the living room a revolving camera that linked to an app on her phone. They would check in on Mantou in real time.

"But what if she goes into another room?" Nate said.

"Then she goes into another room," Keru said.

"We could not go to the alpaca farm," he said.

"I would like to go to the alpaca farm," she said.

As they debated which room their dog would go into, and in each room, which surface she would lie on, a knock came on their door. It was Elena without her husband or child. Her hair was uncombed and wild-like. She was dressed in thin, flowy garments from which Nate had to look away because the light was coming straight through the fabric, and she wasn't wearing a bra.

"Sorry, we didn't see you again yesterday," she said. After the nap, they had, as planned, gone on the hike. After the hike they had, unplanned, taken another nap. Then suddenly it was the next morning.

"Shall we all have coffee again?" she asked sleepily. "Luka woke up asking for Mantou."

"Actually, we're on our way out," Keru said.

"Out?" said Elena, with a frown. "Why out? You only arrived yesterday."

Keru clarified and mentioned the alpaca farm. Elena exclaimed that she had not known about such a farm.

"Do they allow children?" Elena asked.

"Children, but not dogs," Nate said from the kitchen area, as far as he could be from the door but stay within earshot.

"Perhaps we'll see you when we come back," Keru said.

"Yes, perfect, that would be lovely, we would like that very much, especially Luka," said Elena, swaying her hips slightly and biting her lips. The two women stood there awkwardly, said goodbye to each other, and then stood there some more. Only when Keru began to close the door did Elena remember that she was supposed to leave.

Not long after Elena left came another knock. It was Mircea this time, dressed in a vest over a checkered button-down. His hair was combed carefully and slicked back with gel. More so than yesterday, he looked like he worked at the Fed.

He said hello three times. "Hello, hello, hello. Elena was just here and too shy to ask, so I thought I would ask. The farm for alpacas sounds like a good idea. Mind if we came along? If not, please just let us know. We don't want to get in the way of any romance."

The last word made Keru laugh, which made Mircea stare intently at her before saying, "Okay, I had not meant that to be funny."

Each couple took their own car, with Keru and Nate in front, their neighbors following behind. Keru and Nate drove a gray rental. Mircea and his family drove a red Tesla. In the farm's parking lot, Keru admired the bold color and asked how they got it charged. "No need," Mircea said. "At moderate speeds, the Model S can go for three hundred and ninety miles on a single charge," and he had calculated that even with unexpected excursions, they should arrive back in Park Slope with forty miles left, plus or minus five miles. "If not, we call customer service," he said. "Then Elon Musk himself will come rescue us in a helicopter."

"That's funny," said Nate, but not laughing.

"Yes, I know," said Mircea with a serious face.

At the ticket booth there were large signs that explained the crucial differences between alpacas and llamas. First, they were entirely separate species. Second, alpacas were friendlier and didn't spit. A tour ticket included a walk about the farm with a friendly alpaca on leash, and 10 percent off the farm's apple cider donuts. While Mircea and Keru went in to buy tickets, Elena and Nate waited outside. Because Elena was also carrying Luka, Nate offered to carry Elena's bag. "That's so kind of you," she said, passing over the heavy tote. "Mircea never asks such things." As Elena leaned in close to fix the straps of her tote that was now on Nate's shoulder, she touched his shoulder and then, inexplicably, fixed his collar. Relinquishing the collar, she said, "Mom habit," and Nate touched the part of the collar that Elena had just fixed. She was more dressed for the weather than she'd been in the morning. A jacket over a long-sleeve sweater, gray slacks, a scarf. Except for her hands and face, every part of Elena was covered, and Nate tried not to think about her breasts.

"Your wife seems always in a rush," said Elena. "We noticed that she drives fast."

Keru had driven them to the farm as she had to the bungalow. Keru drove whenever she could, citing motion sickness as the passenger.

"Yeah, well, she works a lot," Nate said, and Elena nodded, as if that explained it.

Nate asked if Elena drove.

"In Europe, yes," she said. "But there's no point here. Why retake the test and learn a new set of rules just for two years. I can walk everywhere I need to go."

Nate tried to think of more questions to ask Elena. Was she an artist full time?

"I'd like to be," she said, setting Luka down. Luka called his mother "Mama" and, when being held, buried his head in her hair or whispered into her ear. When Elena spoke Romanian to her son, Nate had assumed Luka replied in Romanian as well. He commented on the child's fluency. He wished that he'd grown up bilingual.

"Trilingual," Elena said of her son. "That was Dutch, not Romanian. My boy sometimes only answers in Dutch."

"Oh sorry," said Nate, embarrassed.

"Don't be. How could you have known?"

Yet Nate thought he should have.

Elena asked if Nate spoke Chinese.

He said, "No, not really." Then, added, "Well, some." But lessons he'd stopped taking a while ago, and he'd not kept up with practice, except to visit his in-laws once a year and sit in their presence. Retired, Keru's father had less to say about fuel cells, and Keru's mother rarely spoke to Nate directly. Though on occasion, she would ask, "Have you eaten yet?" a phrase she only said in Chinese, for it was her most intimate expression of care, and in not realizing he was being spoken to, that he was the recipient of this care, his face would remain vacant, as the eagerness drained from hers.

Elena asked Nate to say something in Chinese.

He tried but it came out gibberish.

"Yes, exactly like I remember," she said, visibly impressed.

He felt like a fool.

When the others returned with tickets, the group made their way to the barn. A handler met them, a lad over six feet tall with the face of a child. His gloved hands looked like clown hands, and he clumped around in big leather boots, half unlaced. The alpacas had enormous eyes, round protruding black spheres that everyone else found delightful but that frightened Nate. He and Mircea each took identical brown ones that the handler said were sisters. The sisters liked to walk together, pressing into each other as if glued. At first Mircea tried to pull his alpaca away from its sister, but the more he pulled, the more his alpaca stalled and bared its teeth. "You see," Mircea said to Nate. "She hates me."

"Alpacas are herd animals," said the handler from the rear. "They need to follow a leader." The leader was Elena's alpaca, strutting out in front, followed by Keru's. The two women were talking and laughing. Lucian walked alongside them, holding his mother's hand.

Mircea and the handler struck up a conversation. The boy was still in high school, a rising senior, and alpacas were his weekend and summer gig.

"Where are you off to college?" Mircea asked, and cocking a half grin, the boy said, "College?"

Mircea tried to catch Nate's eye to imply something, but Nate didn't want to get involved. Mircea then asked the handler what else there was to do in the area, besides hiking, the lake, and this farm. The boy said it was hunting season, and just last weekend, he'd seen a field of at least fifty deer.

"Hunt?" Mircea said, incredulous. "With guns?"

"You could," said the boy, though he preferred bow and arrow.

"Is that right?" Mircea said, and asked Nate if he'd been hunting before. He had, when he was the boy's age and younger, but told Mircea that he hadn't. The boy took off his gloves to scroll through his phone. Then he held his phone up to show Mircea and Nate the buck that he'd shot two weekends ago with his dad. In the picture, the boy, dressed in head-to-toe orange, was standing over the carcass with a smile. "Easily two hundred pounds," he said.

"And what do you do with it after?" Mircea asked.

The boy looked confused. "You eat it."

The group had walked into a large pasture where the alpacas could graze. Here the boy got a call on his walkie-talkie and left them, temporarily, to help out with another tour. With the boy gone, Mircea smiled at Nate and said, "You eat it." Nate said, "Yeah, makes sense." In the middle of the pasture, the women huddled around Lucian and took selfies. About the scene, Mircea said, "How beautiful. Your wife next to mine."

It was impossible not to compare the women. Elena had let her alpaca go and was swinging her arms back and forth freely with the breeze. She then began to twirl, inspiring Luka to twirl, while Keru moved aside, stood stiffly, and held her alpaca on leash with an iron grip.

Mircea asked how long Nate and Keru had been together. When Nate said "Since college," Mircea raised his eyebrows and said, "So you've really been together since like forever." His expression was not one of enthusiasm but of surprise and, possibly, of pity.

"She seems like a good partner," said Mircea, his expression reset to neutral. "You need one person to be practical. I am that person."

They watched Elena and Luka twirl more.

"But how do you keep it fresh?" asked Mircea.

Nate said they had a good routine.

"Routine is the opposite of fresh. How do you not get bored?"

Nate said they kept themselves busy.

"With what?"

"Excuse me?"

"What do you keep busy with?"

Nate blinked and said his work, her work, time off together like now, and their dog.

"Okay, so work," Mircea said, and lightly smacked his lips together, as if pushing out a bad taste. He wanted to know more about Nate, where he was from and what that area was like.

"A bit like here." said Nate. "Rolling hills. Rural."

"And people own guns?"

Nate said, "Some."

"Do you?"

Nate said no.

For which Mircea seemed relieved. "You know what my biggest fear was?" Nate had a guess. "I feared, was truly terrified, that everyone owned guns." But he was glad he knew no one who did. "I guess you have to leave Park Slope to find those people." The last two words caused Nate to bristle.

"I'll tell you what else I don't like about this country. I don't like that you advertise drugs on television. I don't like your tipping culture. I don't like your trash. Trash on the street. Dog shit everywhere. Used condoms in playgrounds."

"Every city has trash," said Nate.

"But Manhattan in particular. That entire city smells like piss."

Nate bristled more.

"What I do like is your return policy," Mircea continued. "I like that you can return anything. Produce you've changed your mind about. A mattress even after one year. If you're the customer, you can complain. That's your right, so everyone complains and everyone returns."

Mircea asked Nate what he liked most about America, and Nate had trouble coming up with a definitive list.

"Most people say the freedoms," Mircea said. "But what is freedom exactly? What happens when one person's freedom infringes on another's?"

Rhetorical questions.

"You must try to live elsewhere, my friend. Even a few months will give you a better perspective. The world is very big." Mircea had opened his arms. Nate had crossed his. "Don't get stuck in one mindset."

Nate was glad to see the handler return and lead them back to the farm. En route, Mircea traded alpacas with Keru so he could rejoin his family. He ran up behind

Elena and wrapped his arm around her waist. He gave her neck a quick kiss.

"Hey," Keru said to Nate, once they'd regrouped.

"Hey," Nate replied. They both watched the other couple stride ahead of them as one unit; even their paces were in sync. Side by side, Elena was half a head taller, and after being kissed on the neck, she turned to kiss her husband on the cheek. If Nate told Keru that they shouldn't hang out with these people anymore, she would want to know why. *Why?* he imagined saying. *They made him feel inadequate about himself, his marriage, and his country; they made him feel like a sham.* Keru would not have accepted such an answer because it was an unacceptable answer. Feeling vulnerable and like a shithead, he asked Keru what she and Elena had talked about. He worried Elena had complimented his gibberish that was truly an affront to the language.

"Oh, you know," Keru said.

"No, I don't know, tell me."

His wife gave him a curious look before checking her phone for the hundredth time.

"We have to leave," she said.

THE HARDWOOD was scratched badly, paint from the door and frame stripped, the welcome mat kicked far away, gone. On camera, Keru had caught their dog digging and now their dog had crazy eyes. A saliva puddle by her paws.

Keru sat on the ground and hugged Mantou.

Nate went to find the welcome mat. To coddle was ridiculous but had he stood there, he would get sentimental, possibly weep. "Disintegration of the pack," said either vet 1 or 2, which Nate thought was obvious, but what could be done about it, except reintegration of the pack, which was not always possible.

When he found and returned the welcome mat, his wife had already dialed the number for the concierge. Already she was describing the damages, offering to send pictures and sounding apologetic. During this time, Nate went to the couch and removed the six pillows. He sat down, put up his legs, and closed his eyes. He could hear a not-so-distant leaf blower, high-pitched and grating. He could still hear his wife, pleasant but fake. "No, no, please take the deposit," she said. "That's what it's there for." She listened and then said, "That's kind of you but unnecessary. We're more than happy to pay." She listened some more and then said, "Well, all right. Thank you and yes, everything is wonderful, we're really enjoying our stay."

The next day came a downpour, and Mantou slept in between them, wedged, her entire body and head buried under blankets.

"I worry she can't breathe," said Keru, looking under the blanket.

Nate said they had to trust their dog to know how to breathe.

Rain enveloped their bungalow. All day they heard the gutters. Hourly, their dog drained her water bowl. When Mantou refused to go outside, Nate had to carry her. They stood for thirty minutes in the rain, him under a weak umbrella, her just outside the umbrella, by a row of eligible bushes, but still, no pee. When they returned, they were soaked. Their dog pressed herself into a corner. "She's drinking but not peeing," Keru observed, and Nate observed, "the umbrella broke." The umbrella had been newly purchased, and when, outside, one side of it totally collapsed on him, he considered chucking it as far as possible, but that would be littering. So he threw the umbrella away properly, in the garbage bin. He put his wet clothes in the dryer, put on dry clothes from their dresser, and reappeared in the living room, where Keru had set the six pillows back on the couch and moved the lounge chair right up against the window to get a better view. Contrary to their dog, his wife was invigorated by torrential weather. She loved overcast skies. Gloom and doom.

She turned to him and said, "You know what Elena told me yesterday? They told me why they took so many naps." Keru said "naps" with air quotes, but Nate still didn't get it.

"She's ovulating," Keru said.

"Oh," Nate said, feeling a flush.

"But what a crazy thing to tell me. Like I would have asked."

"Two makes sense for them," said Nate. "They should probably have two." He'd opened a bag of pistachios and was cracking them directly onto the kitchen island.

"Replacement theory," she said. "Can you please use a bowl?"

"What?"

"To replace the parents. Bowl for your shells."

He was leaning against the island. He didn't bother with a bowl.

"You know what else they like to do?"

"I bet you're about to tell me."

"They like to entertain. They throw parties in their backyard."

"Townhouses have backyards," he said. "That's the one nice thing about them."

"Dozens of people show up. Friends, acquaintances. Teachers from Lucian's school. It's a big event."

"Do you want a party for your fortieth?" he asked. "Is that the hint I'm supposed to get?"

She said they didn't know dozens of people. They couldn't even count one dozen friends.

He said so what, if they had less than one dozen friends, all of them would come.

"Fewer."

His brows scrunched.

"It's fewer, not less."

"Our fewer than one dozen friends will come."

"They're all too busy," she said, picking at her cuticles.

"Have you spoken to one lately? They're like full-time chauffeurs who never sleep."

"If I plan a party, people will come."

"They'll think it's a hassle. They'll want to bring kids."

"I'll say no kids."

"You can't do that." she said, horrified and mouth agape. "No, you have to allow kids, and we have to plan activities for them like face painting. Face painting has become very popular."

"I'll allow dogs, but not kids."

"Why don't you use a bowl?" She cupped her hands together to signal what she meant.

"They're being washed."

"Every single bowl? There's not a single bowl or cup or saucer left?"

"None."

She looked out the window, dreamy. "We should go hiking right now," she suggested. "Imagine being up in the mountains and those clouds."

"Imagine being struck by lightning," Nate said.

"Do you always have to be so depressing?"

"Yes, yes, I do."

They were quiet for a while, then, still facing the window, she said, "I don't wish I had kids."

"Neither do I."

"But sometimes I wonder."

"We would have given up some things."

"To gain others."

"I'm happy with us," he said. "Wouldn't change it."

"I would be happier if you used a napkin," she said. "Just one teeny tiny square for your shells."

He put down a tiny napkin.

A few hours later, the side of their bungalow was hit by a giant steel bat. Or so was the sound. There were no giants in the Catskills. No Paul Bunyans. Nate ran out without his jacket or proper footwear and saw that a gutter had completely torn off, now hanging limp against the paneling. When he came back inside, he smelled a familiar scent. The puddle of piss was enormous and their dog was sitting in it. When Nate swore, Keru said, "Don't yell at her."

"That wasn't me yelling," he said calmly. Then he yelled, "THIS IS ME YELLING."

"I CAN TELL," she replied.

The only way to get their dog out of the corner was for Nate to scoop her up and fold her four limbs together. The position that he'd once deemed her most adorable was now, while she was being held, her most vulnerable. He carried their scooped dog into the bath and set her inside the clawfoot tub. Neither he nor Keru were bath people, so had no use for a tub. But once the water rose to a comfortable level and Nate added a floaty ball, Mantou stood and pawed at the ball. The paw became a pounce. The pounce became a splash.

"You know I wasn't yelling at you, right?" he said as the

pouncing and splashing continued. Their dog appeared
to nod. For certain, she could differentiate between him
yelling at her, which he never did, and him yelling at
the situation, which they didn't have. A situation meant
something was broken, and except for the gutter, the door
frame, a few planks in the foyer, and the umbrella, nothing
was explicitly broken. He had yelled only to show that he
hadn't been yelling, and she had yelled to reciprocate the
sentiment.

THE NEXT MORNING, Mircea came over to check on
them. The gesture was nice, but Nate found it unnecessary. There'd been some rain, not a cyclone. To celebrate
that they had all survived, Mircea invited them to a cook-
out at the pavilion. Nate tried his best to get out of it. He
said they had other plans, but when asked what those
plans were, Nate blanked, allowing Mircea to say, "Then
let's barbecue together like brothers," and to strategically
put out his fist for Nate to bump. Nate had to bump the
fist, there was no choice, and soon he was riding with
Mircea in his red Tesla to a store ten miles away for supplies. At the store, Mircea asked, "What else do we need?
You would know best." Nate went down the aisles. Cole
slaw, potato salad, chips, condiments, corn on the cob, a
pack of IPA.

On the drive back, Mircea played instrumental music.

As the orchestra raged through one of those famous symphonies, he set the Tesla to autopilot and took both hands off the wheel.

"Amazing, beautiful," he said of this capability, both his hands free. He put his fist out again and Nate bumped it. "Land, land, and more land," he exclaimed, gesturing out the windshield. Then he asked if Nate owned land. Nate said no. He asked if his family owned land. Nate said no more than the plot his mother's house sat on. Mircea turned down the symphony and strongly advised Nate and his family to buy as much land as possible.

"Generational wealth comes down to ownership," Mircea said. "In the future those who own the most will have the most."

Nate said owning land or the most of anything wasn't his business.

"Then what is your business?" said Mircea as they coasted to a stop at a red light.

"I teach," said Nate.

"Yes, I know you teach, but teachers are not respected here. Teachers have no power."

From there, Mircea brainstormed ways Nate could incorporate himself as a flow-through entity and develop a consulting firm that gave him more power.

"Then you can work less," he said, "buy property, and take better care of your wife."

"Sorry?" Nate said.

"Don't be sorry," Mircea said, turning the symphony

back up. "We can all take better care of our wives. Me included. It's not good for a woman to work for too long or too hard. Men must work, that is our plight, but in a perfect world, a woman shouldn't have to."

Nate could sense that he was being baited. So for the rest of the drive he disengaged and tried to tune his neighbor out, but he could not tune out everything. To a section of percussion, Mircea pounded on the wheel and said, "I like capitalism, don't you?"

At the pavilion, the women had laid beach towels over the damp chair cushions and were perched precariously at the edge of these chairs. Mircea had gone inside to make spritzes. Lucian and Mantou played by the large, well-groomed hedge. When Mircea came out with the drinks, he carried them professionally on a wood tray. After passing the glasses around, each struck through with a pink paper straw, he went to stand by Nate at the grill, not so close that he would need to do anything but not so far that he couldn't feel the flame.

Keru asked how their yesterday went with the storm.

"Boring," said Mircea. "But dry. We played lots of games."

"We napped," said Elena.

The women smiled at each other, and Mircea seemed confused.

"You nap every day?" asked Keru.

"Almost," said Elena.

"Both mornings and afternoons?"

WEIKE WANG

"They're short. At most an hour."

"Convenient."

"Productive."

The women smiled more and Mircea squinted at Nate and muttered what's going on.

"These are ready," Nate said, setting a tray of dogs and patties on the low outdoor table. "Everyone, grab a plate."

Elena called to Lucian, who came running out of the bushes followed by Mantou. Keru put on her own plate a burger patty with lettuce and tomatoes but no bun. Elena asked if Keru was gluten intolerant, and when Keru said no, Elena said, "Then why skip the bun? The bun is such a joy. Else the balance is off."

"Elena," admonished Mircea, and his wife went back to cutting the hot dog into small bites for their son. Compliments went to Nate for getting the right balance of char on the meats. Not so much that they felt as if they were eating carcinogens but enough that they knew it had been cooked over a real fire. Well done. Luka sat and ate whatever was fed to him. When Elena handed him a napkin, he wiped his mouth first, then his hands. To his parents, the child said some Dutch, some Romanian, and then to Mantou, in English, he commanded very loudly, "Let's go," and off they went to an unoccupied pavilion that was within sight.

"He's very well behaved," said Nate.

"I've made that a priority," said Elena. "I don't want a brat."

"He does misbehave sometimes," said Mircea, and winked at the group. "Other people are just not there to see it."

"When does he misbehave, Mircea?" Elena asked.

"Never, Elena, never," he said.

Elena shooed her husband away but not seriously, then she set her head on the same hand and let her soft hair fall around her face. The women turned to each other and began to have their own dialogue. So Mircea made himself another burger and tried to chat with Nate about sports. "If it's on, I'll watch it," said Nate, but after Mircea brought up cycling, F1 racing, and pickleball (his current obsessions), then moved down to the basics, tennis, basketball, baseball, soccer, he seemed disappointed that Nate didn't have a sport of his own or a hometown team he followed religiously. No fantasy football league. No March Madness. That Nate didn't golf either dealt Mircea another blow. "What do you do, man?" asked Mircea, and Nate shook his head and looked down at his plate. What did he do? He taught four classes a year and ran a small lab with poor funding. His lab had a serious ceiling leak that after months facilities had yet to resolve. Four classes meant four hundred students, mostly premeds with their premed mentalities. He was used to the standard premed, but there was a new breed of student, the entitled type who criticized everything but also didn't want to learn anything but also didn't want to be wrong, the kind to put no effort into the course, fail, and then petition the registrar to have their failing grade reversed, which sometimes Nate had to do, else this student couldn't go on to save lives. It was this hand-holding, followed by the head petting, all the crap, intensified and concentrated, that twenty-some-year-olds thought they could get away with because the college would rather have happy students than happy teachers. Happy students had parents who paid tuition and donated large sums. Happy teachers were not a necessity. So, without meaning to, Nate had become the crotchety older professor who lived in a nice neighborhood with many brunch options, but who still complained a lot about the grind. That's what Nate did. The grind. Both at work and at home. With Keru in Chicago, he was the sole caretaker for their dog, the sole emergency contact. He did all the walks, the feedings, all the trips to the groomers and vets. He had continued with salad eating and slimmed down a bit, but his fear of the great disaster loomed. The disaster had many permutations, the most common being a train nose-diving off a bridge into a frozen lake with him strapped to the front. For sleep, he took supplements, melatonin, magnesium, a cup of chamomile tea before bed. He called his mom weekly, but his wife daily, and when his wife didn't answer, he would wait another hour to try again. In that time, he would do laundry, fold laundry, vacuum the floors, walk the dog again, and answer a dozen emails. Complaints from students, questions from the lab staff, the admin, and his committee work had grown astronom-

ically. He was on at least five, maybe six, different committees, including a committee that oversaw the progress
of other committees. This was expected of senior faculty.
The unending service at the service of the school. Now
Nate knew what emeritus professors meant when they
warned junior faculty, "If you let it, this place will suck
you dry." Hours later, when his wife finally answered from
her corner office with the three monitors, he would try to
sound peppy instead of totally crushed. He would do most
of the talking and present her with a polished observation
from his day. Here, a seashell, busy wife, that was about
what he was trying to achieve. Once it'd been a full moon
in both cities, and he'd said, "The moon is actually a
banana. To see a full moon is to see this banana end
on." Keru was part listening but mostly working. She also
thought the comic moon was made of cheese. "A banana
doesn't make sense to me," she replied, fatigued and without mirth.

"Yeah, I don't do much," Nate told Mircea, because in
part this was true. Compared to his wife, he worked fewer
hours, and compared to his colleagues with kids, he had
fewer life-and-death responsibilities. So technically, he
had ample time to golf.

"I'm just kidding with you, you know that, right?" said
Mircea, and put his fist out to be bumped, which Nate did.

Around this time, the women's voices grew louder, and
Nate heard his wife ask Elena a strange question.

"What's a DINK?" was the question.

"You don't know what a DINK is?" said Elena, shocked or feigning it, and in a voice even louder. Now that the women had the men's attention, Elena said to her husband. "I was just telling Keru that she and Nate are the textbook example of a DINK family. D-I-N-K."

"Yes, of course, DINK," said her husband. "Double income, no kids."

"You don't use that term here?" asked Elena.

"Not really," said Nate.

Elena took out her phone, searched and read what the internet had to say about the word. "The acronym DINK originated in the U.S. in the 1960s. How to use in a sentence. There are more DINK families in big cities. DINK families prefer pets to children. Luxury goods are marketed to DINKs, who have more disposable income."

"So, you don't use it like this?" Elena asked again. "Even though it's from here you don't use it in everyday speech?"

Nate said he never used that word. "Sounds too much like dinky."

"Or dingy," Keru added.

"DINK does not mean any of those things," Elena said, her voice a little shrill. "DINK means only what it means, double income, no kids. Each letter represents a word. It's an American acronym."

"I'm aware now, thank you," Keru said.

"So, it appears that DINK is not a word here," Elena said to her husband. "Which means we must stop using it from now on. We've called a lot of couples DINKs, and now it seems wrong."

Mircea shrugged. "Then we stop using it," he said, and wiped his fingers, one at a time.

"It doesn't bother you?" Elena asked.

"Why would it bother me?"

"What else have we been saying that no one understands?"

Mircea shrugged again. "People understand us well enough."

"We've met lots of couples like you guys," said Elena, turning back to Nate and Keru.

"Who? DINKs?" asked Keru in a tone that was exceedingly polite and ironic.

"No, one Asian, one white, and ninety percent of the time it's an Asian mom, a white dad," said Elena, unironic. "We had no idea there were so many of you until we came here. Now we see you guys everywhere. We see you in commercials for dish soap."

"Which means you must be very popular," said Mircea.

"I don't think selling dish soap means you're popular," said Keru.

"I'm friends with lots of Asian wives nowadays," Elena said. "And they're always stressed about something. Stressed their kids are not getting ahead fast enough. Stressed about other Asians, and that being Asian or part Asian will hurt their kids' chances of getting ahead."

Elena put a hand to her chest. "I feel so bad for these women and am glad Luka won't have this kind of trouble. That's one benefit when you marry within your group. The kids come out more cohesive."

"I'm sure you don't mean what I think you mean," said Keru.

"Of course I mean what I mean," said Elena. "I've spoken to lots of women like you. They all say the same thing, and that's probably why you and Nate want to stay DINKs."

"I assure you, you couldn't have meant what you meant," said Keru.

"Oh," Elena said, startled and looking to both Nate and her husband for help. "Am I not being clear, or did I say something wrong?"

In a cheery, boisterous voice, Mircea said his wife can be too direct sometimes, but she only meant that the raising of any kind of child in America was unsustainable. Even in a year, they'd noticed. "The population is too diverse," he said, holding a half-eaten burger that was dripping mustard. "It's impossible to make everyone happy, and exposing kids to adult issues is not healthy. Race, privilege, class, all that comes later. Kids need to be allowed to be kids." Though he thought the bigger problem in American schools was safety.

"Yes," Elena said, as if safety was what she intended to discuss all along. "You have a major problem. Luka had his first shooter drill last month, and we, as parents, were expected to explain to him why. Arm the teachers, arm the children. Total insanity."

"By you, we don't mean you, specifically," Mircea said to Nate. "We mean you in the general."

"But when you have kids, you'll understand," said Elena, now meaning the you specifically. "We recommend raising them elsewhere."

"Come to Europe," said Mircea, elated.

"Yes, come to Europe," said Elena, similarly elated. "It's the perfect average of East and West. Geographically in the middle. People are happier there. And there are no issues with race."

"That won't be happening," Nate said.

"Why not?" asked Elena, with a casual wave. "Retire early. Build a new home."

"We have a home," said Keru, and that made Nate feel a little better.

Elena brushed some hair away from her face and sighed. "I see that I have offended you," she said. "That was not my intention."

"I'm not offended, Elena."

"You are, clearly."

"I'm annoyed and a little surprised, but please don't assume I'm offended."

The women turned from each other, and Keru asked Nate for the time. Without checking, Nate said late and suggested they start cleaning up. Mircea agreed, but no one got up to clear the food or stack the plates, no one moved. Instead, Elena called her son over and he sprinted to her, with Mantou trotting behind. Luka's pants were dirty from the knees down. What once were bright green corduroy pants were now smeared with black. In English, Elena asked Luka what happened. "Did you fall?"

Luka said no.

"Did you try to climb the dog and fall off?"

Luka said no.

"Tell the truth."

He said that they'd been digging.

"But why?" Elena said, as she began dusting off the boy's pants with loud, forceful pats. "You're not a dog, Luka. You don't dig. Dogs dig because they are dirty, but you are a little boy who is not dirty. You are clean."

When Elena said clean, she emphasized it—her clean, cohesive, trilingual child—and when this child started to cry, she gathered him up and announced that they were going in.

"I'll stay and help tidy," said Mircea.

"Then you'll come inside," said Elena.

"Da," said Mircea, nodding. "Da, da, da."

Luka squirmed in his mother's arms, and when he wasn't released, the cries turned to screams. As Elena was leaving, she shouted for Nate to leash the dog. She didn't want Mantou to follow them to their bungalow or distract Luka from going inside. Instead of the leash, Nate held their dog by the harness. Once Elena and Luka were out of sight, he let her go.

Keru, Nate, and Mircea tidied in relative silence. They divided the leftovers and folded the towels. Mircea stayed longer than he had to, and when the pavilion was spotless and there was nothing left to clean, Keru apologized to Mircea for whatever happened and asked him to pass the thought to Elena. This was out of character for Keru, the apology, the submission, and to witness it, Nate felt a mixture of things, but mostly dismay.

"Don't apologize," said Mircea, standing both feet apart, hands on his waist. "Actually, it's better if you do not. To apologize is to admit to wrongdoing, and you did nothing wrong."

Keru asked if they would see them tomorrow. Maybe they could all finally go down to the lake.

Mircea said they were leaving tomorrow.

"Breakfast then," suggested Keru.

Mircea said they were leaving early to get back to zip code 11217 for the "birthday extravaganza" of one of Luka's best mates. "So many birthday parties, and everything parents must do. It's . . ." Mircea spun his finger around his ear.

"I hear face painting is popular," said Keru.

Mircea said face paint at least you could wash off, but he hated the balloons. "What are you supposed to do with them after? If I pop one, Luka cries."

When Keru offered to get up at sunrise so they could have breakfast together, Nate stepped in to wish Mircea a safe drive back.

"You too," he said, already making his leave, and with one last fist bump. "We very much enjoyed meeting you both. Best of luck."

Had the situation been different, they might have exchanged numbers and proposed to meet in the city. They might have even texted one another and met up once, though probably not twice.

ON SUNDAY, their neighbors left without further notice, and on Monday, the start of their second week at the bungalows, Keru and Nate drove into town for lunch. They took Mantou with them this time and had called ahead to the lunch spot, to see if they had enclosed outdoor seating. The café was remarkably dog friendly and said they would seat them on the patio and bring out a heat lamp for the brisk weather.

Across from the café was a sad Chinese takeout, a staple in every hamlet, this hole-in-the-wall place called Golden Dragon or Jade Garden or Jade Dragon or Golden Garden in the red font of all Chinese takeouts, set against a dirty off-white façade. Keru tried to not look at these places or imagine the workers inside. But from the heated patio, she had a dead-on unobstructed view of this façade, so it was hard not to think that by some roll of the dice, she could be in there sautéing lo mein instead of on vacation with Nate. Under the heat lamp, both her and Nate's faces were red. Mantou had lain down beside the table, and while they waited for service, Nate fed her pieces from the bread basket.

"It's plain white bread," said Nate, reading Keru's annoyance.

"But you never know what else it could contain," she replied. "Trace amounts of nuts, onions, and garlic are toxic."

"Don't take it out on the bread," he said.

For a Monday the café was surprisingly filled. There were many cozily dressed white families sitting inside on quaint wooden chairs. In contrast, the Chinese takeout seemed empty. No one entered or exited, and that made Keru feel guilty for not being over there, ordering large greasy platters of what this country had agreed upon as her people's food.

Keru asked Nate if he thought they led stupid, dinky lives, and he said, "Not this again." Followed by "we do not."

"But why do you think she called us that?"

"Because people like that tear other people down."

She straightened. "They weren't those people and that's not what happened."

"That's exactly what happened," he replied. "We were being judged."

"What happened is I overreacted."

"She overreacted and you really shouldn't have apologized."

"I wanted to apologize."

"Then you enable bad behavior, you enable someone like that to think she's right."

"It was the word *cohesive*, I think," said Keru, as she shredded her paper napkin and rolled the torn-up pieces into tiny white balls. "When I heard it, I jumped. But I don't think she meant cohesive as pure, like pureblood. I think she meant cohesive as less existential, which, I mean, can only be a positive. I wish I were more cohesive."

A waitress came to deliver their sandwiches, and Nate remained silent until this woman was out of range.

"I wouldn't give her that much credit. She shouldn't have said that to us. She shouldn't have said lots of things. I didn't like her or him. And to be honest, whatever time we spent together was a waste."

Keru thought her husband's response was extreme.

"Not extreme," he said. "Appropriate."

The sandwiches were neatly stacked but she had lost her appetite. How meaningless vacation was. To be in a new place with new streets, houses, and people. To have to temporarily adopt new habits, from introducing yourself to strangers to finding a decent place to eat. Removed from routine, even their bickering was different. Which made Keru question why she went on vacation if she didn't enjoy it.

"You could have been less cynical," she told him.

"Adults have to put in effort to make friends," she told him.

"You sound like my mother," he told her.

Keru looked away from him in that moment and immediately he apologized. Then in a gentler tone, said, "Hey, please stop this. I'm begging you. We do have friends, lots of them."

"But have you noticed that they don't invite us to things anymore?" she asked.

"They don't invite us to kid things because we don't have kids," he said.

"I would still like to be invited."

"Well, too bad."

"They don't invite us because they think oh, look here come those DINKs again. What can you possibly talk about with a DINK?"

Nate said he wished he'd never heard that word, and she said she would have a hard time forgetting it.

"The reality is that people with children envy us," said Nate.

"That is absolutely not true," said Keru.

But her husband persisted with this fallacy and his theory. He pressed on in a way that Keru had never heard. Misery likes company, and people with children want the childless ones to join them. People have kids in large part because they think they're supposed to. Having kids is the norm, the capstone to your human experience, and no one wants to be left out. But once you have kids you can't un-have them, so even if you regret it, which no one ever does, you do your part in the messaging, the brainwashing, and haze all those sad, childless people around you to follow suit. A not-to-be-missed adventure. The best job in the world. But what you mean is come over to the dark side, come experience this shitstorm of emotions, submit to the standard, else be deemed broken, incomplete, and be ostracized by all, when the truth of the matter is that not every experience is worth having. Cutting off your own ear is an experience. Snorting cocaine.

"I'm not even going to mention overpopulation," he added. The dwindling of resources. An uncertain future. "I just want to die and be done with it," he said. "I don't want to worry about descendants."

"Okay," said Keru slowly. "We should probably first do our best to separate children from cocaine."

"It's just an example," he said.

"A very extreme example."

"An appropriate example." Then he said he couldn't care less what other people thought, and she replied, with equal emphasis, "But maybe I do."

"Then tomorrow we have kids."

"Not what I said."

While he had finished his sandwich, she had only picked at hers. She missed work where people also had insane theories but at least they were about work. At work, she knew what to do and how to fix problems. She was actually more relaxed dealing with round-the-clock deadlines than having to spell out to a person she loved the difference between children and cocaine. The waitress came to refill their waters and to pack Keru's uneaten sandwich into a biodegradable box. That's what this dog-friendly café was known for. Local produce. Biodegradable utensils and imperfect plates made from pulverized, recycled glass.

"Is this about your fortieth?" Nate asked, after the waitress had gone. "You want me to invite everyone, surprise you, which I'm fine to do. But if I plan a party without your input, you'll find something not to like and then I'll hear about it."

Keru stared at the empty spot on the table where her pulverized plate had been. Her eyes were enlarged, and thanks to the heat lamp, the whites of them orange. "I don't care about my fortieth. I definitely don't want a party."

"Sure, you do. Just admit it."

Keru bent over and put her entire face into her hands. While she was in this position, she said through her fingers, muffled, "I truly don't give a shit about my fortieth, Nate. I just wish you could be a tiny, tiny, tiny bit more cooperative."

He wiped his mouth with the napkin. He spread the napkin back on his lap. "I fist-bumped that guy four times." He counted on his fingers. "One, two, three, four times. I'm not sure how much more cooperative you expect me to be."

After lunch, they stood in front of the café and discussed whether to stroll through town or get back in the car. Keru wanted to go back, Nate wanted to stroll. He held out his hand, and for a few paces she ignored it, so he kept his hand there, open, empty, until finally she took it, and they were once again walking in parallel, with their dog in front.

The rest of town was just the one street that, beyond the café, featured a neat row of shops tailored to a specific clientele. They went into a boutique, perfumed in berga-mot, that sold hundred-dollar beach towels made in France, another boutique that only sold cleaning brushes imported from Germany. Keru picked up a brush with rubber bris-tles in the shape of a hedgehog and asked the shop owner what it was for. "Can be used for anything," said the owner, but when he noticed their sheepdog, said, "though per-forms best against pet hair on a fine wool coat." Fine wool coats were sold in the boutique over, which was adjacent to a fine arts gallery that was only open two days a week, by appointment.

On the walk back, Keru stopped in front of the Chinese takeout. Open twelve hours a day, seven days a week, in-cluding holidays. For a split second, she had an impulse to march in there and tell them. We, the Chinese diaspora, should work less and open more art galleries.

ON TUESDAY, men wearing tool belts came to fix the gutter. They set up a ladder and said the job would be done within the hour. While the gutter was being re-stored, Nate watched from outside and Keru watched from in. Nate had found a lawn chair he liked, and Mantou sat with him, by his feet. Keru had returned the six pillows to the couch and was buoyed among them, uncomfortably. She had her laptop out to answer some work emails but also to pay credit card bills, rent, and to put in the transfer to Nate's mother. Because her mother-in-law didn't work, each month they sent her an allowance that covered what Social Security and retirement did not. At first, his mother was horrified by the arrangement—she could not take money from them and especially not from her own son—but in two months, the horror subsided.

While the roof was being drilled and banged on, Keru inputted transfer amounts and authentication pins. She waited for confirmation pages to load.

In the past year, Keru had been on twenty-three flights. JFK, O'Hare, Minneapolis-St. Paul, back to O'Hare, then JFK, then O'Hare, Minneapolis-St. Paul, sometimes direct to JFK, or LaGuardia or Newark, sometimes back to O'Hare then JFK then O'Hare. Highways to airports. Airports to other airports. JFK to their apartment. O'Hare to a hotel. Minneapolis-St. Paul to a car rental to her parents' place. Keru saw little beyond these areas. She used to fly only economy, but to reduce her hate of air travel, airports, and waiting, she flew either business or first class. In doing so, she accrued points or miles or whatever, and each year on her birthday, the airline she was most loyal to, with whom she had the most points, sent her a small, dismal gift.

In the past year, her mother's medical issues had scared Keru. What would happen to her parents in ten, twenty years? What would happen when both of them began their permanent decline? Her parents neither trusted aides nor accepted moving into a home, and whenever either of them went to a medical appointment, Keru went too, on Face-Time, regardless of what else she was doing. Keru had spoken to lots of doctors on her parents' behalf, translating back and forth words like acid reflux and whole sentences, like "Doctor, I have a scratchy throat and whenever I'm eating spicy potato chips, it feels like I'm swallowing metal tacks." The cancer misdiagnosis had prompted her mother to have grave concerns over their diets. She'd read on some blogs that an Asian diet of fermented vegetables puts you at high risk for everything, and because the Asian diet did not include dairy, Asian bones were far more brittle. Her father asked the doctor how they could live to a hundred, cancer-free, with unbreakable bones, was it to stop eating these vegetables and to eat exclusively cheese? The doctor said the words "energy balance," which Face-Time Keru had to look up via Google, then translate. He also told Keru to tell her parents that a moderate intake of pickled vegetables should be encouraged—he, himself, liked pickles.

If both her parents lived to a hundred, Keru would be in

her seventies. She would have her own doctors and medical visits. She might even be senile.

"Eventually they will have to hire someone," Nate had said.

"The person would have to speak Mandarin."

"Plenty do."

"They would have to deal with all of my parents' habits."

"That's the job."

But perhaps by seventy Keru could clone herself or have an AI counterpart made.

"Eventually they *will* hire someone," Nate said, so sure of this, because his grandparents had hired aides, and his mother would hire aides, because that's what typical families in America do.

Was Keru's family typical? With age, her parents progressed toward the atypical. For one, they'd turned into hermits and took only two trips a year by car. The first to Lake Superior, where they admired the shoreline from a safe distance. The second to a national park, where they took close-up photos of the foliage. The other months, they stayed inside their suburban home and watched Chinese dramas and cooked Chinese food and called their relatives back in China. They told relatives how much space they had in St. Cloud and the very reasonable price of avocados. Keru's parents had no plans to visit these relatives in person. They considered never going back to China at all. The few Chinese friends they'd had in the area had moved south to Florida, a place they also had no interest in going, citing crazy people and mosquitoes. So this was what the end of immigration could look like. Settled, half assimilated, and isolated in your suburban house. Whenever Keru was in St. Cloud, she made a wild suggestion that they go out and do something. She was even open to a drive-through. Keru's father shook his head, citing crazy people everywhere. By crazy, her father used to mean a small set of Americans, but now he meant most of them, the rebels, anarchists, mavericks, the young and uninhibited, the cowboys, boomers, hippies, hipsters, yuppies, the extra-Christians ("evangelicals," Keru told him), the right, left, and middle wing ("I don't have any wing," he told people. "I'm not a bird."). But weren't she and her parents also Americans? So were they crazy to have naturalized?

These calls to the Chinese relatives often involved Keru because the relatives would ask to speak to Keru, whom they had not seen in person since she was a newly-wed. They would ask how she was doing, how old she was now, and since their mindset of her was still a newlywed, jump straight into fatalistic remarks like "So, you're really not having kids." "All that effort your parents went through to raise you in America and you're not passing any of that on. No child to be born in America. What does your American husband think about that? What do his parents think about you?"

Though Keru had decided against kids, these conversations still caused her to cycle through the emotions.

She had a responsibility to continue the lineage, else who would?

But was it her idea to be her parents' only child?

No, it had been Chairman Mao's, then after they left, those early years of insecurity eliminated any chance of her mother sanely caring for a second child.

Fear of what her in-laws have already thought—our son has married someone different. The least this person can do is reproduce.

Fear of what her husband thought deep down, but didn't say. Traditionally, kids keep couples together. They are the glue.

She didn't owe anyone anything.

Except she did owe her parents for feeding, clothing, and not abandoning her.

"Come back to China," said one relative, "where now a woman is encouraged by our glorious government to have three."

When not helping her mother or fielding reproductive inquiries, Keru sat through online work meetings and, from the office window, watched her father in his straw hat exchange one gardening tool for another. By late afternoon, he would bring in a plastic basin of vegetables to be washed, cut, and sautéed for dinner. Keru's father grew enough that in the summer months, they never bought greens at the supermarket. His garden and its ability to feed the family was a point of pride. Why pay for organic when I have organic in my backyard? That her father had immigrated to escape a life of farming but was now farming for fun was the whole rationale behind immigration, to choose if and when you farmed. The farm of her father's childhood was not bucolic. It was not like the alpaca farms of the Catskills, awash with apple cider donuts and hand-woven merch. Her father's family farm had lacked running water, electricity, and proper machinery. Water had to be hauled in wood buckets from a river. The seeding and collecting, done by hand. If the harvest that year was meager, the entire family scrimped and at least one infant per village died. In the early aughts, the Chinese government seized the land to build highways and gave each villager a state-subsidized apartment, in which Keru's paternal grandparents lived until their deaths. So long, shitty farm, her father thought, until, in his retirement, he began to miss his youth, his parents, his siblings, and possibly his homeland. Now their backyard was divided up into rectangles. The Chinese word for farmland looks like this: 田.

What Keru was most proud of was her work, her career, but if she said too much about that, she risked becoming a cliché. Her team and subteams respected her. The firm was inordinately professional. Her Chicago office faced the Chicago River. Her Manhattan office, the Hudson.

And already, she'd said too much. In each location, she had ergonomic furniture and recessed lighting. In both cities, her office required a key card, and the touchscreen elevator to her floor required the same key card, and traversing the white quartz lobby to the bathroom required it too, so during working hours, there was no parting from the plastic badge with a magnetic chip tethering her professional self to her profit-driven firm.

Keru had set out to make money and that was what she'd done, but more and more she sensed that Nate resented her for making money, even though this money helped both them and his mother. Money was her shield, how she measured her worth, and, unwilling to stop making it, Keru weighed how much resentment she could stand.

They were once out with his friends, also teachers, having what she thought was a nice time, until one friend said, thank God his wife was a cardiologist at a private hospital, else on his salary they would have to move out to Wyoming. His wife, the cardiologist, wasn't there. She was at the private hospital, working. A round of unserious comments followed about what it was like to be with spouses, especially female spouses, who made more. "We're not as oppressive as you think," said the only other wife present, a lawyer. To which Nate added that Keru being the breadwinner had been transformative and allowed him to discover the coveted role of house husband.

Everyone laughed at the house husband part, including Keru, though the remark of false modesty stayed with her. For the tone was, who would want to be a house husband, who would want to hold down the fort, while the woman went out and won bread.

An ongoing discussion, debate, argument they'd had:

"Much more than me, you care about money," he told her.

"Someone has to care about money," she told him.

"But sometimes I think you think I don't care about it enough."

Yes, Keru thought, but said no.

"Money is not a be-all and end-all," he said.

"That's one opinion."

"There are other aspects of fulfilling work."

Ah, ideals. And though annoyed, Keru never escalated matters because why do what had been done to her, why strip a person of ideals? But ideals were often diametrically opposed to reality, and what she was witnessing in her husband was the hard crash down. Since grad school, Nate had talked about tenure as if it were some distant, glowing orb that once gotten would henceforth keep him warm. Everyone around him spoke of the orb, his colleagues, mentors, and those who had, long ago, obtained it and become emeritus. The push for the orb had been motivating. He'd published and taught and taught. Office hours, extra office hours, get your office hours here! A few impossible students aside, his teaching evaluations were excellent. He took on more advisees, summer students, and thesis writers than required. But then post-tenure came a deflation, and for months he spoke to Keru not of classes or his research, but of a ceiling leak in his office that facilities claimed was just condensation and had remedied with a black trash bag, duct-taped to the drywall. When the trash bag broke, a gallon of condensation spilled onto the floor, which prompted an alarm, then an annoyed call from public safety to see when, ideally ASAP, Nate could come in to clean up the mess. Keru was home that weekend, so they went in together, ASAP, to mop. Nate's office was located at the end of a dim hallway. The room itself had no windows, and though Keru had visited the office a handful of times, she never remembered it being so drab.

"You should at least ask for one window," she said. "Tenured people deserve better views."

He said no offices on this floor had windows. They were interior-facing offices to accommodate labs that were required to have windows for ventilation. This window in Nate's lab was small and dirty, and faced a courtyard of enormous potential had it not been filled with debris.

"Who cleans down there?" she asked.

Nate said it didn't matter. "No one goes into the courtyard anyway. Everyone here is in lab."

Scientists spoke of being in lab as if it were the womb, a place both terrifying and foreign, that should never be left.

"You could try to talk to someone about the courtyard," said Keru.

"Yeah, okay," Nate said. "I'll go tell the provost right now. I'm sure they'll put in a water feature by next week."

"Doesn't need to be a water feature," she said, controlling her tone. "But you're tenured now."

"So?"

"So they should listen to you more."

He laughed while she stood there, solemn and feeling stupid. She was about to drop her mop and leave so he could be alone with his mess, which he very well deserved, but then she took one more survey of his office—even the incandescent light bulbs were gray—and changed her mind. Academia could be better run, the teachers happier, but whenever she brought this up, Nate would say there were way more science PhDs in the country than offices for them, so any academic with an office should be grateful, and any academic with an office *and* tenure should consider themselves blessed. Nate would also say that he wasn't unhappy. "I'm not unhappy at all. I love what I do." But Keru knew what Nate really liked to do was to overhaul courses and teach students better than he'd been taught. What he didn't like to do was to sit in a windowless room, under a trash bag that filled, at the steady pace of an hourglass, with water. With no other way to catch the incoming drip, they hung up a new trash bag and Nate sent another email to facilities.

From outside, Nate texted her about the finished gutter. He said it looked just like the old one, but shinier. He asked her to come out for a walk. "No thanks," she texted, and asked him to come inside instead so they could have a drink on the deck. He said he and Mantou were going on the walk. He strongly suggested that she join.

"I have emails," she texted, and he texted "You do your emails." Upon which, she threw her phone a fair distance and watched it bounce twice onto the ground, her rage a switch that she'd learned to turn off and on.

ON: I could take my phone to the kitchen and smash it against the quartz countertop until the screen turned to confetti.

OFF: But Keru, then you would have to go to the Apple store and make up some story about how your phone was run over by a car.

So she left her phone there and answered emails by laptop. When the rest of her pack returned, Nate pointed to her phone on the ground and asked if she realized it was there. She said she had not.

FROM HERE, two possibilities:

One: The rest of the week goes the same. Meals. Emails. Two walks a day with the dog. They return to the city refreshed, or so they tell people, but diminished, which they keep to themselves.

Another: A peaceful morning is broken by the crush of gravel from a dust-covered car speeding into the lot. Nate's phone rings, which it never does. Only his side of the conversation can be heard.

"Hello?"

"You're where?"

"Wait, how?"

Nate comes to stand with Keru by the window, and together they watch a man and woman exit the dusty car. Nate mouths some words to her; none she can quite catch. Except her husband does seem frightened and at a loss. "Okay, I'll be right out," he stammers, and keeping the phone to his ear, he puts on shoes and goes out.

Closer, the man begins to look familiar, and Keru thinks how absurd it would be if he turns out to be someone they know. She would never trust vacation homes again. In disbelief, Keru asks the empty bungalow, "That can't possibly be his brother?" A person no one has seen since the funeral and whose whereabouts were better unknown. Once the man spots Nate, he makes his hand into a visor and the other he raises up. Is the gesture one of peace or does he also have a question?

ETHAN WAS SHORTER than Nate but wider. His shoulders were broader and each of his arms was as thick as each of Keru's thighs. He walked with his back hunched and his head forward, like a turtle. He had tattoos of indiscriminate designs along both arms. Similarities: the same shade of brown hair, the same voice, but evidently not the same scent. When Ethan entered, Mantou lunged and snarled at him, but he didn't take this personally and got down at eye level with their dog, got so close that Mantou tucked her tail and sat. "Now that's a good boy," said Ethan, petting her, and Keru said "girl." Keru never knew how to interact with her brother-in-law. She especially didn't like it when they hugged. The hug was so immediate that she never had time to unclasp her hands, so they were crushed between their bodies and pushed into Keru's chest, deflating her lungs. Ethan called Keru little lady or girlie, and that caused her to wonder. First, if her brother-in-law still remembered her real name, and second, why diminutive addresses for petite women were always necessary. Was it for the same reason why Hulk had to be called Hulk?

The woman beside him was his girlfriend, the one Nate's mother had told Nate about, but he had forgotten to tell Keru. She was fit like Ethan and, up close, not as young as Keru feared. Late twenties, early thirties. Dressed from head to toe in athletic wear, hair pulled back in a taut blond ponytail. She nodded as each person introduced themselves and shook each person's hand in a strong and determined way. "Keru like Peru," Keru said, and Morgan said "Keru like Peru" earnestly, like the entire phrase was the name.

After handshakes, Nate asked Ethan how he got through

the gate with the pin pad, and Ethan said the gate was already open. "Someone probably forgot to close it. Nice piece of equipment, though. Sturdy from the looks of."

Keru asked to be filled in. The how and why of Ethan's appearance. "I'm sorry, but can someone—" she started, and with each word, her pulse rose.

"Yeah, about that," Ethan said, rubbing the side of his neck. Their mother had briefly mentioned it, but the address he'd found on his own. Both he and Morgan had the day off. The entire week actually, since their school was on fall break. "Would have called earlier but why ruin the surprise."

The four of them standing in the living room made up the corners of a square.

"What a coincidence," said Keru.

"Who would believe it," said Nate.

"No one," said Keru.

"So it goes," said Ethan.

As Nate showed their guests around the bungalow, Keru opened the fridge to see what they had in the form of refreshments. On one shelf, a head of lettuce and two liters of sparkling water. On another, a half a lemon and a jar of peanut butter. When Nate opened the sliding door to the deck, in came the cold breeze that made Keru shudder. Morgan followed Ethan from room to room, saying nothing about the space or whether she thought it was nice. Ethan addressed Morgan as babe. It was babe this, babe that, babe come check out the view. He asked Nate what the going rate was for a pad like this, and Nate deflected by saying that Keru made the arrangements, he just had to show up. Then everyone was back around the kitchen island, where Keru had set the head of lettuce on a cutting board.

"I could sauté it," Keru said, though the time of day was not mealtime. She simply felt she was required to be welcoming.

"Nah, that's okay," said Ethan, sitting on one of the swivel island stools and turning his body intentionally and exclusively toward Nate. Then as the brothers caught up on whatever, Keru and Morgan were left to interact. But Morgan stayed mostly on her phone, scrolling through clips. To whatever question Keru asked, Morgan gave short, polite answers but did not elaborate. Half an hour passed with Keru learning very little about Morgan except that she worked admin at a prep school, where six months ago she and Ethan had met. That Ethan was part of the grounds team and took care of the equipment was all Keru had gathered. Morgan reminded her of one of her junior associates, a twenty-some-year-old fresh out of B-school who came to every meeting on time, well dressed, and completed every task assigned to her but offered nothing personal of herself. When Keru asked what Morgan liked to do for fun, she said "work out." When Keru asked what Morgan did to work out, she shrugged and said "it depends."

Keru excused herself to go to the bathroom, and from

the toilet she typed a long paragraph to Nate, deleted the paragraph, and finally settled on "Are they staying the night?" "I hope not," Nate texted back, which didn't instill much confidence. When she came out of the bathroom, Ethan and Nate were putting on their jackets by the door and Mantou was on leash. Keru asked where the three of them were heading, and Ethan said the supermarket for actual food and beer. "No offense to your lettuce," Ethan said to Keru, though the lettuce belonged to Nate. Nate asked her if it was all right he went, otherwise he could stay. Keru was surprised by how tender he sounded, and how helpless. Perhaps he wanted Keru to save him and be the controlling wife that his family had pigeonholed her to be. She would not, of course. She would see how this played out. Ethan clucked his tongue and slapped Nate not so gently across the chest. "We're going," Ethan said. "Let's roll."

Once the boys were gone, the space went quiet. Theoretically, each woman could have gone about her own business and pretended the other one wasn't there. But then Morgan's fitness watch began beeping, and she said it was time for her to work out.

"Can I come?" asked Keru, with some latent desire to connect with Morgan. The only-child thing was also kicking in, for if the brothers could go off on their own terms, then maybe Keru and Morgan could find theirs.

"I run fast," said Morgan. She'd run 9.75 miles yesterday. She hoped to do the same today.

Keru said she couldn't run that distance—9.75 miles, holy shit. But she would try to follow her for three.

By the first mile, Keru had fallen behind. She had to stop, put a hand to her chest, bend over, and pant, with saliva running down her chin. Morgan had run ahead and looped back. "I think I'm going to die," Keru said, and, jogging in place beside her, Morgan assured her that she wasn't.

Between gasps, Keru said, "You. Don't. Know. That. My. Heart. Could. Explode."

"Distract yourself," said Morgan glibly. "Think about something else."

By mile two, Keru had to stop twice more and go through the same ordeal of organ resetting. She asked Morgan how red her face was from her soon-exploding-heart.

"Not red at all," said Morgan. "You look festive and full of life."

As Morgan jogged in place, her leggings made a swish-swish sound that was constant and oppressive. At some point, she began jogging backward, facing Keru, to interrogate her. She asked Keru how many times she exercised per week, and Keru lied, but even this fake number was too low for Morgan. "Daily exercise is crucial," she said. "You must adhere to a regime or you will always be behind."

While running, Keru was incapable of thoughts. She couldn't think about anything except how painful running was and how stupid it was to continue a voluntary activity that caused enormous pain.

By the end of mile three, Keru couldn't speak anymore, so she gestured at Morgan to keep going without her. Morgan seemed grateful and sprinted off. In less than a minute, she became a speck on the horizon, and Keru could no longer see her. On the walk back to the bungalow, Keru stopped to sit on a rock. Several cars slowed when passing her. A few honked. One car stopped fully and a concerned white woman rolled down her window to ask if Keru was all right.

"I'm fine," Keru said with a big wave. "Just bad at running. Trying to catch my breath."

The concerned woman became less so and told Keru the rock she was sitting on belonged to the house behind it and was technically private property of those owners. She advised Keru not to run this close to the road, anyhow, and not to run alone. "It's dangerous. Unsafe. Cars drive fast here, especially around turns." She reminded Keru that hunting season was in full swing, so they hit deer all the time.

"Thanks," said Keru to the advice and to being likened to a deer. The satisfied woman drove off.

THE COUCH WAS A PULLOUT, so without much discussion it became clear that Ethan and Morgan would spend the night. Dinner was surprisingly uncomplicated, and even Keru felt at ease. They shared the cooking duties and made large bowls of pasta and salad, with garnishes. "I don't like blue cheese," said Nate as he and everyone else watched Ethan crumble it into the salad. "You'll live," said Ethan in their mother's voice, and everyone laughed.

They drank beer, wine, and after dinner, Ethan made a round of cocktails with a full bottle of whiskey he brought in from the trunk of his car. Nate read the front and back of the bottle, sniffed the whiskey, and seemed surprised, as Keru was, that his brother had brought something to share. They sat around the coffee table, Ethan in the arm-chair and Nate and Morgan on the couch. Nate had moved the throw pillows off to give him and Morgan more room, while Keru sat on the floor against one of these pillows.

Keru asked Morgan if she had siblings.

Morgan said two brothers.

"Older or younger?"

"One older, one younger."

"That's cool," said Keru uncoolly.

Morgan glanced at Ethan, then back down at her phone.

"I hated being the only child," said Keru. "I often found myself alone."

"But you can't choose your own siblings," said Ethan.

"Accurate," said Nate.

"Oh, fuck off," said Ethan, laughing.

This was weird, Keru thought, but not unpleasant. The four of them together, and eventually Morgan would come out of her shell. In some idealized future she and

Ethan marry. Then they all hang out more and become friends. Keru had friends, but now these friends had spouses, kids, and complex schedules that involved the kids. Moreover, she felt her female friends pitied her but pretended not to. When discussion dove into motherhood, Keru found it near impossible to participate. She also did not cook, a failure that she now felt was acutely female. Several women had stopped working and, provided for by their husbands, with the help of a nanny or live-in parents, said in front of Keru but not directly to her that it was nice "to finally mellow out." Keru had no interest in mellowing out. Mellowing out seemed like a kind of death.

Ethan raised his glass and the rest of them followed. "Cheers," he said, and the rest of them repeated. Then, after they each took a large sip of alcohol, Ethan asked Nate if he kept up with news from their hometown. Nate said he didn't, and Ethan asked why not. Nate asked why should he.

"'Cause we grew up there, doofus," said Ethan.

Nate, the doofus, shrugged.

"You know Brett?" Ethan began, and Nate said no. "Sure, you do, Brett from Little League, nice, normal kid. Came over once. Well, Brett can't work anymore on account of his seizures, so now he's on disability. Thought he was done for but crazy thing is that the state pays you more on disability than you would make holding down a minimum-wage job, isn't that crazy?"

Nate said, "Yeah, crazy."

"You know Tim?"

"Not really."

"Tim from wrestling. Lettered in wrestling. Ran for class president. Anyway, Tim married Amber. Three kids, maybe four. Last winter, she took their kids and left him, so he tried to kill himself by letting his car run in the garage. Amber had him institutionalized, and now the state pays for his treatment, his food. The guy never has to worry about bills again. Even if Amber divorces him, he won't have to pay alimony. Isn't that crazy?"

"Crazy."

"You know Dawn?"

Nate had no idea who Dawn was.

Dawn won homecoming Ethan's year, started college but dropped out. "Good-looking girl, happy girl. Miscarried twice, but eventually got pregnant by Zach, had the miracle child, and everyone was joyful except now the child has issues. Attention issues. Behavioral. She divorced Zach. Zach's changed, you see."

Nate asked who Zach was.

"Zach, a street over. Parents left him the house. No mortgage. Totally paid off. Zach from marching band, used to be a real nerd but now sells drugs," or so Ethan suspected, or so their mother suspected. Nate asked why their mother thought that. Because cars went in and out of Zach's driveway at all hours. And they never stopped for more than a few minutes.

Nate said hmm.

"You know Sarah? Sarah had a stroke, then gained about two hundred pounds. Josh?" Who everyone in school knew was gay but who never came out. "Hepatitis, very sad. Cody?" High all the time thanks to Zach, bipolar they think, lives with his mom. "Johnson?" Johnson was the last name but neither Ethan nor Nate could remember the first. "Stepped out of the car while his sister was driving it, while the car was still moving, broke his neck, died instantly. And what about Donny?" Donny actually left and tried to make something of himself, but wound up with two baby mamas and was now living in a camper in his parents' backyard to avoid paying child support.

By the end of these updates, Morgan had gone to the bathroom and Keru was thoroughly depressed. Fine, Nate's family had come from white trash, but why did the trash have to be dragged out, discussed, and enumerated? Her mother-in-law had this problem, too, of going on and on about the tragedies, as if living with misfortune was honorable and listing them out gave her strength.

The last time Keru visited Nate's hometown was for the funeral. She'd sat in the living room across from Nate's mother as she looked through albums of photographs and wept. The living room was brown, as it had always been. Brown carpets thick with cat dander. Brown sofas sunk in at every cushion. Wood paneling. The entire house also smelled of this color, of groundwater collecting underneath. When Nate's father was still alive, Keru had offered to help them renovate, new flooring and fixtures, a fresh paint job in every room, to which Nate's father had said, "We like it here, Keru, we wouldn't change a thing." Either this was pride or he was speaking the truth, that they did like it there, since the house was also their home.

The sense Keru had of where Nate came from was paralysis and stagnation. Cycles of hardships plagued everyone, but there was nothing to be done about it, nothing they could change, and no one could leave. To leave was to tap out and to escape the hand you'd been dealt. Who did you think you were to do that? What false power did you believe you had? Nate's parents had never criticized Nate for leaving, but they neither encouraged it or commended him for doing so. In Nate's childhood home, Keru had trouble grasping what being American was. Stagnation was the opposite of immigration. Her own parents had uprooted continents. Her own mother hated old things. But for rooted families that never changed zip codes, the norm was to have a weathered living room like Nate had, that once was the space of comedy and bright mornings, the father in the kitchen flipping pancakes and whistling, the mother flipping picture books for her boys on the new couch. The goal then was to enshrine this room forever, even in its decay.

Ethan swirled his empty drink glass, just an ice cube left. He asked if Nate remembered the mine, the mill, the rubber factory, the abandoned church, churches, the dismantled train station, rails buckled and overrun with weeds, the defunct aqueduct where they used to play.

Nate remembered all these places.

"There's no work," Ethan said.

"Because no one wants to work," said Nate.

"People want to, they just can't," said Ethan.

Nate looked off with what Keru recognized as indignant apathy. He loathed talking about where he'd come from. He loathed being asked about it.

When Morgan came out of the bathroom, she had taken her ponytail down and let her hair fall around in a stringy mess. She rubbed her eyes, yawned, and on her way back to the couch, tripped over a throw pillow and needed to be steadied. With Morgan in this state, the brothers became agreeable again, and together they moved the coffee table and pulled the couch out while Keru found sheets. Everyone said good night to one another, affably and in turn. In the bedroom, Mantou found a hard corner to sleep in that was not the corner with her memory foam bed. In the bathroom, Keru brushed her teeth like a normal person while Nate brushed his teeth like he was scraping paint off cement.

THE FOLLOWING MORNING, when Keru went into the kitchen, Morgan was already up and in her ponytail. She was about to go for her run, and though still physically broken from the day before, Keru was determined to join.

"I think it's better if you rested," said Morgan, head tilted in sympathy. "You look tired and a little sore."

Keru said she wasn't sore at all. Also, how could a person *look* sore?

Morgan hesitated but waited for Keru to change. They ran on the sidewalk, and when there was no sidewalk, they ran on the road. An incoming car sounded like an incoming missile, and when the missile went by, they stepped off the road and ran in the wet grass of someone's front yard. No car stopped to scold them and no homeowner yelled at them to get off their lawns. So, as a human shield, Morgan wasn't bad. At an intersection, they stretched, and while stretching Keru told herself that she had to push. If she wanted to keep up with Morgan, she would have to completely exhaust herself and deplete the tank. As they took off, Keru forced herself to sprint beside Morgan, who was jogging at a comfortable pace. Morgan sped up, too, but was still not exerting herself and, truthfully, looked quite bored. Somehow Keru managed to say, "Let's race to the next intersection," and Morgan shot her an indestructible smile. Then she was gone. Keru called after her, but the speck was too fast. In that moment, the ground under Keru gave way and she felt her ankle bone bend 90 degrees and touch gravel.

She'd rolled this ankle before, lots of times. She had weak ankles, like her mother, which she now remembered was the main reason she never ran, and her mother never ran, and there were no Olympic runners in the family.

Keru grabbed her ankle, howled, lost her balance, and fell over into the grass. By the time she stopped howling,

Morgan had reappeared. She tried to help Keru up, but the bad foot gave out.

"Can you walk?" asked Morgan.

"Clearly not," said Keru.

And the bungalow was too far for her to hobble back.

"You should probably call your husband," said Morgan in a way that made Keru think she didn't remember his name.

"Right, I should probably call Nate."

"Ethan won't be up yet. So there's no point in my calling him," said Morgan.

When Nate picked up, for a full minute Keru could only hear Mantou barking, which meant their dog had climbed into bed and was sitting on Nate's chest. Her husband sounded groggy and had not even realized she'd left the house. Eventually the news was conveyed. Nate was coming to pick Keru up.

The women sat together in the grass, and for Morgan's company, Keru was grateful. Alone, she would have been terrified. To the few cars that slowed down and flashed their lights, Morgan smiled and waved blithely. One pickup truck honked, rolled down the window, and gave them a thumbs-up. Out of mere politeness, she encouraged Morgan to keep going.

"No way," Morgan said. She would stay until Nate came.

Keru looked down at the swollen joint between her foot

and leg. Right after the sprain, the ankle had seemed white and shrunken, but now it was angry, red, and throbbing. Keru could feel her heartbeat through the ankle. Like her heart might have slid down her torso and become this ankle, *lub dub, lub dub.*

"I was only trying to impress you," Keru admitted. "I didn't want you to think I couldn't keep up."

"Impress me?" said Morgan, a laugh quickly followed by a frown.

"I just mean I wanted you to like me. I wanted us to get along and have things to do," said Keru, unsure if she was making the situation better. "Ethan's never introduced anyone to us, so I just thought. It's silly."

Not only did Keru feel silly, she felt pathetic and old. Confessing a need to be liked. Pathetic.

Morgan picked at the grass around her, plucked a handful of this private property, and tossed it away. "Look, you and Nate seem like nice people. And I like Ethan. But we're not committed or anything. So I wouldn't take it too seriously."

"Oh," said Keru. "You're not taking it seriously?"

"At least I'm not," said Morgan.

"But is he?"

Morgan thought about the question, then said, "We're just hanging out, it's chill."

"So he brought you along to hang out? Or to chill. Or whatever." Keru had a new edge in her voice.

"I mean I don't need to be here," said Morgan, with much more attitude than a moment ago. "I never asked to come. It was his idea, not mine. I'm just a bystander."

Bystander to what? Keru felt like a silly woman, but now she felt misled. What did Morgan know or not know? What had Ethan told her?

"Did he tell you something about us?"

"What?" said Morgan.

"Did he tell you something specific about me?" Keru thought about the axe frequently, but it was more a passing thought, an annoyance, like oh there scuttles a rat. In any case, the incident was years ago, and Keru had not thrown an axe since. She was recovered.

"No, not really," Morgan said.

"Which is it?" Keru asked. "No or not really."

Morgan blinked.

"He must have said something." said Keru.

"He did not," Morgan said in that firm way of being done.

Once again, Keru saw in Morgan that junior associate about whom Keru knew nothing and who was therefore capable of anything, like laughing at her behind her back. Keru gave no reason for her associates to dislike her, but maybe everyone did. Everyone pitied her. Everyone knew about the axe. She imagined Morgan telling her real friends, that guy I'm fooling around with took me to meet his sister-in-law, who kept wanting to run with me, but had no real talent for exercise and seemed to have no friends. Pathetic.

"He should be coming soon, right?" asked Morgan about Nate, setting her fitness watch to start her run anew and standing up to stretch. There was an indentation in the grass where she'd sat, several bald spots where she'd plucked. Keru stared down the empty road and said, "Yeah, any minute now. Sorry for the wait."

IN THE CAR, Nate saw the ankle and said they should get it X-rayed. Keru didn't want an X-ray, she just wanted to lie down. When they got back to the compound, he helped her hobble through the parking lot and pavilions, up the porch steps, and into the bungalow. The couch was still pulled out, with Ethan still on it, casually sprawled, drinking coffee and playing on his phone. "Hey guys," he said, without looking up. Nor did he look up while Nate got ice and two Advils or while Keru put the ice on and took the pills. She studied her brother-in-law, though. Studied his ease, his total lack of concern. She studied the way his thumb flicked across the screen, as if flicking off insects, and the rough way he handled his coffee mug, streaked in brown and set on the side table without a coaster.

"Ethan," she said.

"Yo," he said, looking up.

"Use a coaster."

He said he hadn't seen a coaster.

She pointed to the stack.

Then once a coaster was in place, once she had witnessed its placement with her own eyes, she walked slowly, with Nate's help, to the bedroom, where she told Nate she needed complete darkness. She needed to see nothing. He drew the curtains and closed the door and stuffed a bath towel under the door to block out the light.

Hours passed with Keru awake. She could hear noise from the group, and midday Nate came to her door and said that they were going into the town for lunch, to that quaint sandwich café popular with the white folks, and did she want anything, like a sandwich or a combo platter from the takeout place next door? When Nate peeked in, Keru had pretended to be asleep and let her mouth hang open. "She's out," he said to the rest of the group, and soon they'd gone.

For the next twenty minutes Mantou barked, with both paws up on the windowsill. These were either barks of sheer terror—"You've left me behind. You've left me behind. You've left me behind"—or she was saying, "Bring me back roast beef."

From bed, Keru called her mother, who was also in bed with a bad ankle.

"Guess what, Mom?"

"What?" her mother said. "You're not having a nice

time? I told you two weeks of doing nothing was too long. Everyone gets sick of everyone with that much time."

"What's Dad doing?"

"Gardening."

"Okay."

"Okay."

Her mother had to get back to her Chinese drama and Keru had to get back to her own.

Eventually she got up, limped to the kitchen, made herself a Manhattan, sat in the armchair, set her iced big foot up on the ottoman, and drank the Manhattan. As she drank, she could feel her ankle and head swell simultaneously. When the rest of her clan returned, Nate asked to see the ankle, and when she took away the ice, there was no ankle anymore, just a mound of red the same width as her calf.

"We should really go to a clinic," he said, and Ethan agreed. But what did her brother-in-law know? Morgan looked up clinics and the nearest was closed, but they could drive forty minutes to an ER.

"No ER," said Keru, and lifted up her Manhattan, which was her ER. She asked for more ice and Advil. Her husband obliged.

That evening, Keru was well taken care of. Without having to leave the armchair, she was presented, around dinner time, with a bowl of turkey chili, dolloped with sour cream.

Small talk and pleasantries.

The chili, delicious.

The sour cream, a nice touch.

Downtown was quaint.

That little sandwich shop.

That shop that only sold brushes.

The vibe.

So quaint.

Quaint AF.

Then Nate asked Ethan how he liked landscaping at the school. Ethan was indifferent to it, but it kept him active most days and the pay was decent.

"They make you coach any?" asked Nate.

"Nah," said Ethan. Not that he would have wanted to.

"So, you'll be there awhile?" asked Nate.

"Nah," said Ethan. He didn't care for the people. Morgan glanced up from her bowl at Ethan and said, "Thanks for that." Her expression was surly, joyless, and glum. Ethan nudged her leg with his foot and said, "Not you, babe." "By people," he meant the kids, the students, and most of the teachers, but Morgan had already moved her leg away. "They all think they're special," he added about the students.

"Course they do," said Nate, but went on to acknowledge that as a professor at a private college, he also contributed to this "pedagogy of specialness."

"Pedagogy," said Ethan. "Who taught you to use fancy words?"

Nate suddenly looked embarrassed. Ethan smirked and then said, "My advice is don't drink the Kool-Aid."

Keru cocked her head at this expression that she'd not heard in a while.

To drink the Kool-Aid was to accept death.

To drink the Kool-Aid was to become sheep.

But as a child, all she wanted to do was drink Kool-Aid, which her mother never bought, for all the right reasons mothers had—too colorful, and sugar-filled, and with only so much a week to spend on food, why spend it on junk?

Kool-Aid. SunnyD. CapriSun. Whatever junk her class-mates drank, she wanted to as well.

To immigrate was to drink the Kool-Aid. "Who doesn't want to be an American?" says the immigrant. "The best country in the world." Then once you're here, you have to make the one-way trip worthwhile. You have to convince yourself and others that your decision was right. Look, the space, the geographical belts, the very reasonable price of avocados. Look, our new and improved home. But in truth, immigration was a zero-sum game in which the alternative could never be known.

Had her parents remained in China, she might have too. The Keru in China might never have spoken English or gone to Yale. Never married a man in a fish fin or raised with him a sheepdog or be sitting here with his id-iot brother. But she might have felt less like an aberration, with everyone around her the same as her, studious only children, dressed in the same white-and-blue uniforms, red scarfs around their necks for good grades, marching in straight, neat rows off to school.

As Keru considered how much metaphorical Kool-Aid had drawn people like her parents to come live here in the land of guns, crazy politics, and stereotypes, forever stranded between two worlds, Ethan announced that he'd recently had an epiphany. His stint at a private school has given him firsthand experience on inequity, and it irked him that the rich simply get richer doing absolutely nothing. What he'd noticed is that those with the most wealth owned things. They owned businesses, land, houses, other companies. They had entire buildings at the school named after them. So Ethan now wanted to be part of that, to build something from the ground up.

"Personal fitness has become incredibly profitable," said Ethan. "People like individualized attention." A buddy of his was a freelance PT and easily made six figures. The buddy had so much business he now turned people away. All through flyers and word of mouth. The kind of gym he wanted to open was small, exclusive, tailored to personal training. The space wouldn't need to be huge, just large enough to store equipment and fit a private class. He wasn't interested in rows of treadmills or ellipticals. He was interested in community.

While Ethan talked, there was just the sound of spoons clinking against the bowls. Morgan finished her chili first, drew her knees in, and took out her phone. She didn't seem like she was listening to Ethan or anyone anymore. Once Keru realized that this poor woman's presence was mere buffer and they would never see Morgan again, she set her bowl aside and soon the tomato sauce had the sheen of coagulated blood.

Ethan planned to open his gym in their hometown. Towns like theirs were dying. They were losing people fast, and he wanted to rebuild. He would then also be closer to their mother, and wouldn't that be convenient if he was just a short drive away?

"Hoping to go in on this together," said Ethan, only to Nate. "We don't have the capital yet, but if we invest together, returns are guaranteed."

Nate had made salad and was now scooping some lettuce up and eating it off his fingertips. Then he asked about the check that Ethan had received from their father's life insurance. A check Ethan informed Nate had long been cashed.

"I'm coming to you first," he continued, "because I'm letting you have the first opportunity."

"We're not well versed in gym investing," said Nate.

"And you don't have to be," said Ethan. "You can learn anything on the internet." Besides, he knew enough already, had plenty of connections and could manage the funds. Ethan said the high end, the absolute cap that might be required, though they were certain it would not require as much, but to prepare Nate for any surprises, like renovations of the space, equipment purchases, the first months of low membership, general overhead, licenses and permits, was around ninety-nine thou.

"Uh-huh," Nate said.

"It's a lot," Ethan admitted. "But we'll make it back in a year or less, guaranteed. And it doesn't have to be a lump sum." They could contribute however much they wished at first and then, seeing how things go, add more in later.

"How do you know it's guaranteed?" asked Nate.

Ethan mentioned his friend again, in the park, who posted his own flyers and dragged uphill and downhill, each morning, a trolley of weights. Six figures.

"But have you seen the numbers?" asked Nate. "Have you worked them out yourself or with an accountant?"

"Logistics come later," said Ethan. "Once we find the space, the rest will come. Most importantly, we wouldn't be keeping all our profits. We intend on donating most of it to fix up the parks, the public pool, reseed the soccer field, start proper after-school activities, bring in new businesses and new jobs."

"You're going to do all that?" said Nate.

"That and more," said Ethan. "So, what do you think?"

Nate said no.

"No as in you don't think we'll do what we set out to do or no as in you won't even consider helping us."

"We're not in a position to help that much," said Nate.

Ethan asked Nate if he was sure about that. "Because Mom seemed to think different."

The laugh Nate produced was maniacal. Keru had never heard her husband laugh like that. "Yeah? She told you to come directly to me now? What else did she say?"

Ethan seemed thrown off by the laugh too. He looked at Nate strangely. "We didn't talk details. But just thought I'd ask."

When the brothers came to this impasse, Keru asked about a small business bank loan, given how community-centric these plans were. Ethan said those were more complicated, and with his credit score, he would have to take on higher rates. It would take ages to pay off.

"That's how the system gets you," he lamented. "They punish you for not being rich enough. Then they money-gouge you for trying to give back."

It struck Keru as ironic that her brother-in-law was complaining about a system that, had he made a sincere effort in, would have been kind to him, forgiving and generous. Ethan had his challenges, but so did everyone, and mostly Keru just wanted to shake him until a better, less tragic epiphany landed in his head.

A FEW HOURS LATER, in bed, a still awake Keru told a still awake Nate that they could put the money into a trust.

Nate said, "A trust. What trust?" The man was known to scam his own mother.

Her husband had his eyes closed but began to breathe quickly. Keru counted his breaths until they had slowed.

Then she said that while she recognized all those factors to be accurate, perhaps tomorrow they could have a calibrated discussion about the possibility of giving said profligate brother not ninety-nine thousand dollars, but some smaller amount, with the promise of more, conditional on the opening of a legitimate gym.

"There won't be a gym," said Nate. "Not now or later."

"Are we angry about the request itself or that it's the reason he came?"

"I'm not angry," Nate said, and didn't sound angry. He sounded jaded, dismayed, hurt, let down, resigned, but not angry.

"He did come and see you. He put in that effort," she said.

"If he brings it up again tomorrow, I won't acknowledge it. And if Mom brings it up, I'll stop talking to her."

"That seems extreme."

"Your word of the week." Nate turned on his side, his back to her. "You don't even like my family. Don't worry about this."

True, she did not like or trust his family, but Nate had only one parent left and a brother was still a brother. Now Keru understood that his presence required money, that there would always be requests for something, and that most likely he would take their money and run off. But as with her husband's student loans and her mother-in-law's allowance, she felt she was expected to help, else she would be disparaged, resented, and in the long run, lose Nate.

When Keru told her parents about the allowance, they'd been unsurprised. "You should have stepped in a long time ago. You're not poor anymore," her mother said. "And the more you help the better his mom will think of you, of us, and of Chinese people in general." How could Keru represent all Chinese people? One point four billion people, how could Keru accomplish that? She knew she wasn't poor anymore, but why did everyone feel an explicit need to remind her. She was "not poor" by design. She had not skipped through a meadow and come across a pot of gold. Yet these were her duties. To assimilate, work nonstop, make money, and provide. As such, Keru had no way of differentiating her filial duty to her mother-in-law and her complicity in fueling this woman's delusions. His mother wished to believe the money came from Nate, and Keru had never disabused her of that since the transfer did come from their joint account. His mother believed that an allowance from your son was not a handout; that other people got handouts and those who did should own up to it. Was this white privilege or misogyny or xenophobia? Could it possibly be all three? Tax season caused the most difficulties. Each April, Nate's mother would fume to Nate about paying taxes because she did not believe Congress was doing a good enough job. Why did she have to pay taxes when so many lived here for free? Those living here for free included but were not limited to the thousands pouring through our borders, each woman strapped with eleven or so newborns. His mother hated the phrase *white privilege.* "It's not about race, but class," she said. Class, class, class, like she was taking them all to school. For her, privilege was private education, a second home upstate, summers at the beach, winters in the mountains, horseback riding, an endless staff of cleaners, nannies, tutors, and help. By these metrics, she and her late husband had no privilege. Where were their scholarships back then for being working class? Where are those scholarships now? Where was the help for troubled Ethan? "If there's anyone who's privileged, shouldn't it be you guys? You and Keru have good incomes and take nice vacations. You have enough in the bank to share with all of us. And most importantly, you don't have kids."

Snippets Keru only heard in Nate's retelling. His mother was careful never to bring up these concerns with Keru. In person, they were so civil, too civil, and given how many topics were off-limits, all they could discuss were the pets. But Keru was no moron; she knew how much closer mother and son had become, perhaps out of necessity, like the last two people left on a raft. His mother still spent holidays with her sister, but Nate said he might go down next year, for Thanksgiving, the first in over a decade, though he set no expectation for Keru to come.

"I would have to go if you went," she'd said.

"But Mom would understand if you couldn't."

"Couldn't or wouldn't?"

He said that made no difference to him. Besides, he would only go down for the day. "I wouldn't betray you like that."

The word *betray* rattled Keru, and for the first time she thought to ask, "What have you been telling your mother about us? What does she think of me?"

"I don't tell her everything."

"You shouldn't be telling her everything."

"She thinks you're very capable."

"She's never given me a chance. She's never tried to understand me."

Nate rubbed the sockets of his eyes, and afterward the skin in that area became swollen. "She thinks you're very capable. I think you're very capable. Every living person who's ever met you thinks you are extraordinarily capable."

Which to Keru did not sound like a compliment.

Though she was capable. And stubborn.

The reason she made everything look hard was that everything was hard. "Ease is an illusion," as her mother had once said repeatedly.

The other reason was that she would never stop trying; she could not. The immigrant mindset, perhaps. Survival, and from that experience she knew that whatever her mind was set to, she would accomplish, and whatever it took, she would get there, and against all odds, she could fend for herself. Since rage had fueled much of her competency, it would continue to fuel it and be channeled into righting the imbalance she and her husband were in. She did not always understand Nate's despair or his preoccupation with disaster. This vague, intangible dread only worsened when she was away. So the solution was to be away less, so she could be physically present to right the course. They would go down for Thanksgiving together. They would take better care of each other and their dog. The unit had to be protected, and she would protect them. They were codependent, she and Nate. Without her, he lost grounding, but without him, she could be relentless and too focused. Yesterday, she'd fed their dog a banana and realized it's been months since she fed their dog a treat or poured out the kibble or filled the water bowl or been with their dog alone. She broke off bits of the banana, set them in her palm, and as Mantou gently took them, she also licked Keru's palm. It occurred to Keru then what her husband had meant about the moon. The moon was a gigantic banana, hung up in space, rotating through all the possible shapes. The crescent moon was the full banana. The full moon was this banana lying down. Keru smiled as she considered how big this banana would have to be, Neil Armstrong slipping on its peel and saying "Houston, one giant slip for mankind." Also, wouldn't all the dogs go crazy for it if they knew, and was that why wolves howled at the moon?

THEY WOKE to sounds from the living room, conversation, heated, and the front door opening, then closing. When the door closed, it slammed, so the entire house shook, and by the time they got out there, Ethan was up but Morgan was gone. From the window, Keru could see Morgan marching down through the grass to the gate, with her bag of things. Nate asked his brother what happened. Ethan said nothing happened.

"But where's she going?" asked Keru, watching Morgan strut to the gate, drop her bag, and take out her phone.

"Wherever she wants," said Ethan.

"It'll take her ages to get a car. Don't you think you should go out there and talk to her?"

When Ethan said he wasn't doing that, Keru told Nate to. "Just go ask where she wants to go, we'll take her."

"No need," Ethan told Nate. "If she doesn't want to be here, she doesn't have to."

Keru's ankle was still defective, and she couldn't put much weight on it, but when neither Nate nor Ethan did anything, she stepped out on the porch, on one foot, and shouted, as loud as she could, Morgan's name. Morgan looked in the general direction of the scream, but made no effort to scream back. Then a car pulled up to the gate, and she threw her bag inside and quickly crawled in herself. Then the car drove off.

When Keru returned, Ethan and Nate were at the dining table, face-to-face, a decorative but empty fruit bowl between them. Keru could hear. "Was it a fight?" and "Nah." "But you'll talk to her." "Depends." When Keru sat down at the table, the three of them made up a triangle. But the brothers were still talking and didn't notice Keru take her place.

"You shouldn't have brought her to begin with," said Nate. "You shouldn't have come at all."

Ethan winced and scratched his earlobe. "My brother, ladies and gentlemen. My own flesh and blood."

"What's wrong with you?" asked Nate.

"Many things," said Ethan.

"I'll tell you what's wrong with you."

"It's nothing I haven't heard."

"You're an opportunist."

"And you're the golden child."

"You're manipulative, irresponsible, petty."

"True, I'm no people pleaser."

"You're lousy to have around. The worst kind of family. No one should help you. No one should show up for you. You deserve to be alone."

"Fighting words," said Ethan.

"Meant them," said Nate.

Ethan made a face that was like, all right, then swiftly reached over the table and tried to hit Nate on the side of his neck. Nate saw the hit coming, dodged, and swung back. This went on for several seconds, with Mantou circling the table and barking, and when neither man managed to hit the other properly, Keru formed one hand into a fist and pounded her fist onto the table like a gavel. She pounded it until she had everyone's attention.

"We are not going to behave like this," she said. "I will not accept it. Sit down."

They sat.

Keru truly believed they had to come out of this more functional. If functionality required more of her, then so be it. In the not-so-distant future, it might just be the three of them plus dogs. With parents and friends gone, they were bound to look after each other and put up with each other's bullshit. This future was bleak, but it could also not be. They could try their best to be functional people instead of desperate ones. They could choose function over dysfunction.

"Starting today, things are going to be different," Keru said.

"I like how things are," said Ethan.

"I like them too," said Nate.

"I don't," said Keru. "So starting today, things must and will change. You can either listen or leave."

"Seems like we know who the boss is," said Ethan. "Seems we all have to do whatever she says."

"Then you're free to go," said Keru to Ethan, staring at him and daring him to, and under her direct gaze, like that of a high beam, Ethan did not rise from his seat and did not go, thus allowing Keru to continue and lay out a possible future for them, one filled with lies, mistrust, contempt, scorn, holiday after holiday ruined, more vacation homes to burn, years of absence, regret, infighting, and blame, until they fell apart, destroyed one another, or died. Was this the family that any of them wanted? Were they going to wallow and get nothing done?

She asked these questions to two bowed heads and answered that this was not the future she wanted. She did not come here for such a future. She refused to wallow. Know what you can change, what you cannot. Do not waste what you have been given, and do not lose hope. But moving forward required mutual respect.

"Is there mutual respect?" she asked, and Nate looked up and said there was. She asked Ethan if there was mutual respect, and Ethan looked down and said there could be, but he also didn't like being scolded, he wasn't a child.

"If you see me as a threat, I become one," she told Ethan. "I am not trying to be a threat."

Once Keru finished speaking, some agreement was reached that a bleak future should be avoided. There was discussion of when they should see one another again and what the boundaries were for functionality to resume.

Keru said by year's end she would turn forty, at which time a gathering might happen. The party itself did not matter to her, but if she was now expected to helm the ship for forty more years, a celebration with people and cake, but no candles, could occur. "You can come or not," she told Ethan, who said, with weary compliance, that he would consider it and let them know. After this tentative plan was set, Ethan rose from his seat and stepped backward. He pushed his empty seat in and took his leave. Then it was just Nate and Keru at this table. Together they formed a line. A line moves toward infinity in either direction. A line hangs on by a thread. They did not look into each other's eyes romantically, but seriously. Their beautiful dog sat between them. They took turns petting her beautiful head. He asked after the ankle, and she'd forgotten about the ankle. She touched it and found it to be less tender. He asked if they should go to the hospital. She replied not yet.

ACKNOWLEDGMENTS

To my family and friends, this book would not exist without your continued support, care, and gentle prodding about the book. To Joy, Sarah, and the team at Riverhead, thank you for the conversations, the guidance, and the unwavering belief in these pages. Michael, I agree with you—living with a writer is a challenge, so thank you (I love you), thank you for rising to the occasion and telling me to keep going.